"He took something from me."

His posture was so rigid, Mia thought he would snap. "You don't have proof my uncle is the man you seek," she said. Her heart pounded so hard the blood roared in her ears.

"I found the evidence I need." Linc refused to look at her. "I found what he took from me. No one else had the means to take the one thing that mattered to me."

His wife. The blood drained to Mia's feet, leaving hear as cold as death. Her body had never been found... Seven years ago in the explosion... Her own car accident had been seven years ago... She remembered nothing from that day or from her entire life before. It had been day after day of trying to remember. Night after night of dreaming things that made no sense.

Air would not enter her lungs. The porch shifted and swayed beneath her. Her vision narrowed until it encompassed nothing but his eyes. "You think I'm your wife."

Then the spinning sucked her into a vortex that grew deeper and deeper until everything else vanished.

DEBRA WEBB

BROKEN

TORONTO NEW YORK LONDON
AMSTERDAM PARIS SYDNEY HAMBURG
STOCKHOLM ATHENS TOKYO MILAN MADRID
PRAGUE WARSAW BUDAPEST AUCKLAND

The loss, pain, challenge and triumph portrayed by the characters Mia Grant and Lincoln Reece in this story is very close to my heart. If not for the talented, patient and compassionate folks in physical and occupational therapy at SportsMed in Huntsville, Alabama, I might not have learned to use my right arm and hand again. Thank you all for caring and for never allowing me to give up.

ISBN-13: 978-0-373-69550-8

BROKEN

Copyright © 2011 by Debra Webb

www.Harlequin.com

Printed in U.S.A.

ABOUT THE AUTHOR

Debra Webb wrote her first story at age nine and her first romance at thirteen. It wasn't until she spent three years working for the military behind the Iron Curtain and within the confining political walls of Berlin, Germany, that she realized her true calling. A five-year stint with NASA on the space shuttle program reinforced her love of the endless possibilities within her grasp as a storyteller. A collision course between suspense and romance was set. Debra has been writing romantic suspense and action-packed romantic thrillers since. Visit her at www.DebraWebb.com or write to her at P.O. Box 4889, Huntsville, AL 35815.

Books by Debra Webb

CAST OF CHARACTERS

Lincoln Reece—He is an Equalizer who has nothing to lose. Everything was lost to him seven years ago the day his wife, Lori, died. When his former LAPD partner tells him his wife is still alive, will Linc dare to hope and risk that emotional devastation a second time?

Mia Grant—She is a simple woman of approximately thirty years of age who began her life a mere seven years ago. When a stranger arrives in her small town claiming she is his wife, her carefully constructed world turns upside down.

Slade Keaton—He is the enigmatic head of the Equalizers, a private investigations firm that ensures justice outside the law as often as inside. Keaton has secrets that even the woman who loves him is afraid to uncover. Those secrets involve the Colby Agency, and Keaton just keeps getting closer and closer.

Vincent Lopez—He is Mia's godfather. She calls him her uncle. He saved her life and ensured that she received world-class medical care. But is he really a hero?

Gloria Lopez—She is Mia's adopted aunt. She is a kind, compassionate woman who would do anything for Mia... perhaps even keep secrets that might tear Mia away from her.

Teddy Stewart—He would like Mia for himself, even if he has to use a gun to keep her away from the man he believes to be a dangerous stranger.

Juan Marcos—He was the most wanted drug lord on the West Coast until he was targeted for assassination by a competitor. His assassination cost many lives, including Lori Reece's.

Jim Colby—He is the son of Victoria Colby-Camp, head of the Colby Agency. He is glad to help out the new owner of his former firm, the Equalizers. But Jim has a hidden agenda. He is certain Slade Keaton has his eye on the Colby Agency. The only question is, why?

Chapter One

One more drink and he was out of here.

Lincoln Reece nodded to the bartender, an unspoken order for another of the same. He exhaled a lungful of relief that his latest assignment was successfully behind him.

There was no greater rush than the one that came with victim vindication. No one should be allowed to get away with taking advantage of little old ladies. Particularly not a man operating under the guise of the Good Book. The three elderly widows on whose behalf Linc had acted had gotten back the deeds to their homes, and the unsavory counterfeit minister who'd done the swindling was behind bars without bail, awaiting the next step toward prosecution.

The bartender left the glass on the counter and moved on to the next patron without missing a beat.

Linc took a long swallow as he turned on the bar-stool to watch the Friday-night crowd. Most nights he was not on assignment he was here. He liked it here at Hazel's House. The music was low enough for conversation, not that he ever talked to anyone. Best of all he could slide deep into oblivion and walk the three blocks to his rent-by-the-week room. No one cared who you were or what your deal was here in Hazel's House.

Unless you dogged out the Cubs or the Bulls.

A table overturned on the other side of the room. Shouting broke out as bodies collided and fists swung. Linc leaned back and propped his arms on the counter to watch the show. A woman hollered that she didn't belong to no man. Ah, the other reason the occasional brawl broke out in Hazel's House. Jealousy.

Bouncers swaggered over to clear up the debate. Linc rotated the stool, turning his back to the ruckus. He didn't need any trouble tonight. He was here to chill. The last time he'd let his old cop instincts guide him he'd spent the night in lockup. His boss had gotten the charges dropped within mere hours of Linc's call.

Slade Keaton, head of the Equalizers, had a seem-ingly endless supply of resources. Linc downed the rest of his bourbon. Keaton was a decent boss. Linc hadn't enjoyed anything about a job—and he'd had several—or about life in general for seven years. Working as an Equalizer gave Linc the closest thing to satisfaction he'd experienced in that time. If you could call existing to work a sense of satisfaction.

Linc laughed, the sound little more than a growl in his throat. Not living...just existing. Sad. So sad.

"Thought I'd find you in a place like this."

Linc recoiled. What the hell? His bleary gaze cleared instantly. But his brain reacted a little more slowly. He blinked to banish what was no doubt an alcohol-induced hallucination.

The man laughed, near loudly enough to drown out the blues melting from the speakers mounted in the joint. "That's priceless." He leaned in close. "What's it been? Five years?"

Linc gave his head a mental shake as he looked at the man with the gray hair, matching scraggly beard and laser-beam blue eyes. Mort Fraley. Enough long-exiled memories abruptly bombarded Linc to leave him shell-shocked.

Anger rammed his gut. "How'd you find me?" Linc hadn't seen or spoken to anyone from his old life since he'd given up on the idea that she might still be alive. *She.* He couldn't even bear to think her name, much less say it out loud.

Mort slid onto the stool next to Linc. He raised a hand to the bartender, pointed to Linc's glass and held up two fingers before turning his attention back to Linc. "I can't believe you asked that question." His eyebrows reared upward. "I've been a cop for thirty years. Besides," he said as he picked up one of the two glasses the bartender dropped off, "I was your first partner. I taught you everything you know. Finding you was amateur hour, amigo."

Linc knocked back a long swallow. Didn't do a thing for the tangle of emotions roiling in his belly. He swiped his mouth and met his mentor's gaze. "How long've you been keeping tabs on me?"

"Since the day you hit I-10 and put the City of Angels in your rearview mirror."

That too-familiar searing pain roared through Linc's chest. He decided to cut to the chase. "What do you want?" Linc had moved around a lot the past five years. He'd landed in Chicago just six months ago. Six weeks later he'd hired on with Keaton as an Equalizer. L.A. was a place and time he had no desire to revisit.

Mort contemplated the question for an irritatingly long time before answering. "I retired last year." He shrugged. "Finally started to travel the way the wife has always wanted."

A smile attempted to crack Linc's defensive disposition. "You been driving a motor home around the country like one of those old geezers who retire to Palm Springs every year?"

Mort made a face. "It beats sitting around the house waiting to die of boredom."

Linc shook off the moment of nostalgia. He didn't deal with that sentimental stuff anymore. "You two passing through?"

Mort glanced around the crowd, then turned a deadpan expression in Linc's direction. "Is there someplace quiet we can go?"

That face was another blast from the past Linc could have done without. The impulse to tell his old friend and mentor to get back in his motor home and hit the road pressed against his chest. But Linc knew this man…really knew him. Mort wouldn't have gone to the trouble to find him if it wasn't important. And he sure wouldn't be hiding behind that mask he saved for interrogations.

"You dying or something?" The possibility added another layer of uneasiness to the churning in Linc's gut.

Mort pushed off his stool and threw a bill on the bar to cover the two drinks. "I saw an all-night diner down the street."

Linc dropped the cash for his own tab tonight. "I know the place."

Mort jawed all the way to the diner, catching Linc up on the old narcotics team, whether he wanted to hear it or not. But he'd put that life behind him; he wasn't going back for anything. As if to defy his determination, Linc's bum leg ached, adding a noticeable hitch to his gait.

The instant they slid into a booth Mort ordered a round of coffee. Black. This was serious.

"You know the wife always had a thing for country music." He chuckled before sipping his coffee. "All I've heard for thirty years is Nashville, Tennessee. 'I want to go to the Opry.'"

The coffee was hot and smelled strong enough to have been brewed at breakfast that morning. Linc fingered his cup. "Nothing wrong with having a dream." He'd had dreams once. Before he'd realized that it was better not to care. A man had nothing to lose if he owned nothing, cared about nothing. Especially dreams.

"Nothing at all," Mort agreed. "I figure I owe it to her for sticking with a narcotics detective for thirty years."

The abrupt lure of much-needed caffeine got the better of Linc, and he sucked down a gulp, then gritted his teeth at the bitterness after all that smooth bourbon.

"Last week," Mort went on, "we drove from Music City to a little Tennessee town named Blossom, of all things, outside the nursery capital of the world." He harrumphed. "Little village cluttered with antique shops, historic homes and nurseries filled with every sort of blooming bush and tree you can think of. As you can imagine, I was in heaven."

A deep, guttural laugh burst from Linc's throat. He couldn't remember the last time he'd laughed—a real one, anyway. "I'm surprised you got out alive."

Mort didn't meet Linc's gaze. He stared into the coffee cup, both palms down on the table.

A choke hold tightened around Linc's throat. Something was definitely wrong here.

"The wife and I took one of those hokey historic tours." He shrugged. "You know, where they show you the oldest houses in town and whatever it is that puts the place on the map. Like the oldest Holly tree in the country. It's on the National Register of Historic Places, by the way. But none of that got my attention."

His instincts thumping like the subwoofers in a drug-dealing pimp's newest ride, Linc braced. Whispers, images from seven years ago seeped past the wall he'd built to block those memories.

Mort looked directly at Linc. "It was at the pink antebellum house, the Dowe house, that I saw *her*."

The urge to run hit Linc hard. He shook his head. "I don't want to hear this." He held up his hands. They shook. "I gotta go."

Mort grabbed him by the arm before he could

slide from the booth. "Sit." He nodded to the seat. "Listen."

When Linc hesitated, Mort pressed, "You know me." He searched Linc's eyes, winced at what he no doubt saw reflected there. "I wouldn't be here if I wasn't sure."

Linc jerked free of Mort's hold and dropped back into the booth. He leaned across the table. "My wife is dead. You're the one who forced me to accept that fact!"

Mort heaved a heavy breath. "I can't argue with the truth." He nailed Linc with an unwavering stare. "But I know what I saw and heard."

Her body was never found. But then neither were the remains of most of the others who died that day. Only two survived. A thug. And Linc. Not a day had gone by since when Linc didn't wish he'd died, too. If he weren't such a damned coward he would have pulled the trigger one of those mornings when he'd stuck the muzzle of a gun in his mouth instead of coffee.

"Her face is a little different."

Linc scrubbed at his jaw, stroking the scar that slashed across his left cheek. "Then you could be wrong." Not *could* be. He *was* wrong. *She* was dead. Linc's wife was dead. It had taken two years for him to face that fact. Then he'd spent the next five running from the reality.

Mort shook his head. "It's her. The voice was hers. The way she moved. She goes by Mia Grant. The folks I talked to said she's lived there for about six years. The whole town loves her. But not one of them could say where she'd come from. I checked out the name. There was no Mia Grant matching her description prior to six years ago."

Linc couldn't do this. "I appreciate that you went to all this trouble to let me know." He was done here. If he sat here a second longer he would explode.

"I watched her restoring plaster molding in one of the houses on the tour."

Every single cell in Linc's body ceased to function.

"Her hands. The way she held the tools." Mort moved his head side to side again. "It's her."

Lori had been a tough cop. A narcotics detective. One who'd skipped her way to detective because she had uncanny instincts and an amazing ability to fall into character instantly. In her off time she loved driving around looking for old homes. She'd searched for months to find the perfect historic home before they'd decided to buy. A real fixer-upper. They'd hit a wall when it came to restoring the plaster. Hiring it out would have cost a small fortune. Lori had set out to master the skill of restoring plaster and she'd done it so well, her work had made a California home-builders' magazine.

A dash of hope combined with the agony that was churning deep inside Linc. He shook his head. What Mort was suggesting was impossible. "She's dead," Linc said. If she had survived she would have found a way to come home. No way would she be hiding out in some small Southern town. She had loved Linc. She wouldn't do that. His mentor was clearly growing senile or suffering from dementia.

Mort was the one to throw up his hands this time. "Believe what you will, but know that I watched and analyzed her for days before I came here."

Linc wanted to shake him. The man was pulling out all the stops. "Mort, I—"

"It's her."

Linc shook his head. "Why would she do this?"

The resolution in Mort's eyes held steady. "If you don't believe me, go see for yourself. What've you got to lose?"

Nothing. The agonizing truth sank deeper into Linc's bones. He had lost everything seven years ago. The day his wife died trying to bring down a major West Coast scumbag, Linc had, for all intents and purposes, died with her.

"Just go," Mort urged. "Lori's alive."

Chapter Two

"That guy is back."

Mia Grant smoothed the plaster she'd just spread with her trowel before turning to her friend. "What guy?" She knew perfectly well what guy Tina Marie meant, but Mia had learned quickly to defuse the teenage girl's fancies and suspicions or suffer the consequences.

Tina Marie made an impatient sound. "You know, the one who's taken the tour twice already this morning." Tina Marie crowded closer. "He watches your every move, Mia." The girl's eyes sparkled with mischief. "He's kind of cute." She glanced toward the guy in question. "Like a character from a Brontë novel."

Mia smiled. Tina Marie had been hooked on

Wuthering Heights since her freshman year of high school.

Mia watched the man wander around the parlor as if he hadn't seen it twice already. He was handsome in a brooding sort of way. Tall, with dark shaggy hair, a beard-shadowed jaw. The jeans and black shirt he wore fit like they were designed just for him. Nothing like the off-the-shelf jeans guys around here wore, but then there were no fancy stores in Blossom. Even the slight limp and the scar marring his jaw were attractive in a forbidden sort of way.

He turned toward her as if he felt her staring at him. Tina Marie gasped and rushed over to actually do her job at the souvenir counter. Mia held the stranger's stare. If he wanted something, now was as good a time as any to find out what. No need for him to pay the ten bucks for a third tour.

She stepped down from the ladder, swiped her hands on her apron and walked right up to him. "Is there something I can help you with, sir?"

His eyes were blue. Deep, dark blue. She couldn't help noticing, since he continued blatantly staring so intently at her. That old scar trailed up from the corner of his mouth to just beneath his eye on the right cheek. Mia suppressed a wince at how close he'd obviously come to losing that eye and forced her attention back to his gaze. He still watched her.

"Mia Grant?"

She blinked, surprised, not that he knew her name but at the deep, gravelly sound of his voice. It provoked a tiny shiver. Strange. "That's right." She extended her hand. "And you are…?"

His stare dropped to her outstretched hand. "Reece." He lifted those fierce blues back to hers. "Lincoln Reece."

He folded his hand over hers and squeezed firmly before letting go. His hand was wide, strong, long fingered. An unexpected shock rippled through her, and she pushed away the silly reaction. "How can I help you, Mr. Reece?"

"The house on Magnolia."

Mia nodded. "The nineteen-ten folk Victorian. The Reid house." She knew the one. Once upon a time it had been a grand place. That neglected beauty had been empty for nearly two years.

"Yeah, right. That one." He shoved his hands into his pockets. "How much do you know about the house, Miss Grant?"

The man was nervous. Really nervous. Quite odd. "It's a lovely old home." She lifted a shoulder in a vague shrug. The house was for sale. Maybe he was interested. "Needs some TLC. But it wouldn't be that difficult to bring her back."

"I was told you do restorative work." He glanced at the ladder a few feet away.

That explained why he'd been watching her.

"Some. I specialize in restoring plasterwork." As foolish as it sounded she was a little let down that he was interested in her work and not her. She shouldn't be surprised, though. There hadn't been so much as a movie invitation in the last year. She would have to work hard to recall her last real date. That was the trouble with small-town life. Everyone knew everyone else. Labels were stamped quickly. No one would dare risk hurting poor Mia's feelings…or crossing her powerful uncle.

The hands came out of Mr. Reece's pockets and he seemed to relax. "I'm considering buying the place and I wanted an estimate on the restoration work." His gaze traveled down to her sneakered feet and noticeably slowed moving up her jeans-clad legs and over her apron and T-shirt. That he lingered on her breasts prompted another shiver.

Flustered, Mia hesitated. The first hint of uneasiness slithered down her spine. "I'll have to check my calendar. This time of year folks are focused on taking care of things around the house." That wasn't exactly true, beyond exterior maintenance and upgrades—none of which were her specialty—but this man was a stranger. A girl couldn't be too careful.

"Chandra Green suggested I speak to you."

Had he read her mind and provided a reference? In any case she relaxed a little. Mia would be calling

Chandra. It wasn't unusual for real estate agents to recommend local contractors. Not that she was a real contractor. More a handywoman who'd marketed the only skills she possessed. "Chandra knows my work."

Mr. Reece pulled a business card from his shirt pocket and offered it to her. "I'll be in town for a few days. If possible, I'd like to make a decision on the house before I leave."

Mia studied the card. Only his name and number were printed there, not one other detail. "I'll call you this afternoon." No point making the man wait too long. If Chandra gave him a thumbs-up, Mia would jump on the job. She could use the work. There weren't that many historic homes left in town in need of her particular restoration speciality.

"That's perfect. Thank you." He stared at her another moment, then turned and walked away.

Very strange, Mia thought. She tucked the card into her apron pocket and walked to the window to watch Lincoln Reece stroll down the sidewalk toward the town square. Where was he from? He possessed no discernible accent. There was nothing to glean from the way he dressed. And certainly not from his card.

As if he'd once again sensed her thoughts, he stopped and turned back. Mia eased to one side of the window to prevent being spotted. He studied the

Dowe house for at least half a minute before resuming his trek toward the center of town.

As she watched him blend into the pedestrians strolling on the tree-lined walk, she winced at her reflection in the glass. She looked a mess. Wisps of hair had fallen loose from her ponytail. She had plaster smeared on her T-shirt and jeans, despite the apron. Not exactly a professional presentation.

"So? Who is he?" Tina Marie demanded as she peeked over Mia's shoulder.

Mia jumped. "His name is Lincoln. He's looking at the Reid house. Chandra suggested he check with me about the plaster repairs."

Tina Marie chattered on, but Mia didn't get a word she said. The funny shock she'd experienced when she and the stranger had shaken hands still puzzled her. Spending so much time in these old homes, she met lots of strangers, tourists mostly. She'd never had one do that to her with a bear hug, much less a brief brushing of palms. And Reece was by no means the only handsome or enigmatic man she'd encountered, on or off the job.

"I'm taking a break," Mia said, interrupting her friend's lengthy supposition about the stranger. "I'll be back in fifteen."

Mia skirted the dozen or so tourists oohing and ahhing over the dining room and cut through the kitchen to reach the back gardens. She moved away from the house to avoid interruptions by those wandering the blooming paths of the gardens, slid her cell phone from her pocket and called Chandra.

According to Chandra, Reece was a serious potential buyer.

"So this guy is legit?" Mia asked.

"Definitely," Chandra assured her. "He's ready to buy and he doesn't need financing. The man absolutely insisted I show him all three of the historic homes in town that are for sale. On Sunday no less."

Another surprise. He hadn't looked like the type with that kind of money or that sort of determination. "He picked the Reid house over the others?" It was by far in the worst condition.

"He preferred a fixer-upper," Chandra explained. "Wants to get his hands dirty."

Actually he wanted to get Mia's hands dirty. "I guess I could call him."

"Be sure you do, Mia," Chandra urged. "You know how slow the housing market has been. I could really use the sale."

Things were tough all over town. "You can count on me." That was what folks did here in Blossom. They helped each other out.

After Chandra finished her drawn-out monologue about how handsome and mysterious Reece was, Mia grabbed the opportunity to end the call. Mr. Reece had better watch himself. Chandra had been divorced for three years. She had bemoaned the slim pickings hereabouts for that same time. Reece fit the Realtor's image of the perfect man—hot and loaded.

Mia would call Reece. But not for a couple of hours. She could use the work but she didn't want to appear desperate. Fair pay wasn't too much to ask, even in this economy. If he pegged her as desperate he'd start trying to negotiate her prices in the wrong direction.

She propped her hands on her hips. This could be a godsend. Maybe she'd get that new stained-glass window for her bathroom after all. Not to mention a little cushion in her bank account.

Her uncle had offered to replace the window ten times. But Mia was a grown woman. She could support herself. Her uncle had done far too much for her already.

The journey had been long and arduous but Mia Grant was fully capable of standing on her own two feet. She smiled. That had not been the case just a few years ago. Funny how a person's darkest hours could seem so far away and not so bad after all when looking from well on the other side of tragedy.

Mia liked this view a whole lot better.

Chapter Three

1:00 p.m.

It was *her*.

Linc braced his hands on the bathroom wall and peered into the mirror. It was Lori.

Her face was different, the nose mainly, like Mort had said. But Linc had watched her move. Every move. The way her hands stroked the plaster. The way she arched her back. It was her.

The eyes…Lori's eyes. Pale brown, almost gold. She wore her shiny brown hair the same. Long, silky. He'd know that mussed ponytail anywhere. While they'd talked he had studied her face. The cheekbones were so much like Lori's, with only the subtlest changes. The brow area was different, but the lips were exactly the same.

He was certain it was her. But she hadn't recognized him.

His gut clenched. He'd watched for the faintest flare of recognition in her eyes. Nothing. But when their hands had touched, her pupils had flared. That alone couldn't be attributed to recognition. He was a stranger. For all he knew this Mia Grant might respond to all strangers, especially males, in that manner. According to one of the guides at the Dowe home where she'd been working, guys were wasting their time setting their sites on Mia. She was untouchable. Of course, the guide was young, twenty-one or twenty-two maybe. Lori—Mia—had turned thirty this year, though she looked closer to twenty and always had. The youthful image had worked to her advantage in undercover work.

Doubt nagged him and Linc pushed it away. *It was her.*

How was that possible? Everyone on that damned yacht had died except Linc and one of Juan Marcos's thugs. No one else had survived. They had searched for survivors and bodies for days. Only a few who'd been on board had been found. They had been so deep at sea it was impossible to even hope to find them all.

When the recovery efforts were halted, Linc had lain in the hospital counting the hours and days until he was released. Then, with the help of a private team, he'd searched the water for days more. He'd gone to every hospital and clinic in a hundred-mile radius. Nothing. Not a single other survivor had been treated in the area.

Eventually he'd given up.

Linc stared at his weary reflection. Maybe he'd lost his mind. No. If that were the case, then Mort was crazy, too. Mort was sure this woman was Lori.

But Mia didn't remember Linc.

Amnesia? Chances were she had sustained a head injury in the accident. If the amnesia had been merely traumatic or only partial, she'd be past that now. Was it possible that all she needed was the right mental nudges? He needed to talk to a specialist. He had no idea what the ramifications of a memory loss so profound and long-lasting could be.

The other screaming question was how she had gotten here.

This was nuts.

Linc wrenched the faucet handles, letting the water flow from the tap. He bent down and washed his face. *Think! How can this be?*

He grabbed a towel and scrubbed it over his face. If she would take the job he'd offered her, he could buy some time to figure this out. For the past seven years he hadn't given one damn about material possessions. His paychecks had gone into the bank. He'd lived on bourbon and the occasional sandwich. Buying the Reid house wouldn't be a hardship.

Staying here for as long as necessary wouldn't be, either.

His cell vibrated. He snagged it by two fingers and slid it from his front pocket. The number on the screen told him it was the boss. "Reece."

"Have you made contact?" Keaton asked.

Slade Keaton ran a tight ship at the Equalizers. He cared that his investigators were good to go professionally as well as personally. But he never stepped over the line. In recent weeks, though, his personal involvement with his staff had changed considerably. When Linc had first come on board, Keaton had been all but anonymous.

"I spoke to her briefly." Linc forked the fingers of his free hand through his hair as he moved to the bed and plopped down. "It's her." The words echoed over and over in his brain.

"The dental records were faxed to my office. I'm loading them into a PDF. I'll send them to you shortly."

"Thanks." Not that he had a clue how he would accomplish the comparison just yet.

"You're certain there are no living family members?"

"None. Both her parents passed away when she was in college, and she's an only child." Linc wished like hell he could go the DNA route, but there was no comparison sample. Fingerprints would have been the simplest method, but the gas leak explosion at the L.A. Hall of Records a year after the accident that had taken her life—or so he'd thought—had decimated all official files, including the DMV files. The obliterated files hadn't meant anything at the time, but now he couldn't help wondering if the two incidents had been related.

"No prints, no DNA." Keaton made a sound that reflected his own skepticism. "Sounds almost like a well-thought-out plan."

Anger stirred in Linc. "She wouldn't have done that." No way in hell Lori would have set up her own death to get away from her life...from Linc.

"That wasn't an accusation," Keaton assured him. "Only a statement of fact."

Linc rubbed his weary eyes. His chest tightened to the point of restricting any possibility of a breath. "Point taken."

How the hell was he going to do this?

There was no quick and easy method. He needed time and access.

"If you require any other of my available re-sources—"

"I'll call." Linc hesitated. "Look, I don't know what I'm doing here." He rubbed his eyes with his thumb and forefinger. "This is...crazy."

"Maybe," Keaton agreed, "but there's only one way to find out."

That was the bottom line. "If I were working this as a case, I'd be looking into any Marcos connections in the area." Even though Juan Marcos was dead. Like Lori. "If this is my wife, Marcos had something to do with it." No damned question. Marcos had been the biggest drug lord on the West Coast. Many had tried, but no one had been able to get close to him, much less bring him down, until Linc and Lori infiltrated his organization.

"I'm on it," Keaton guaranteed. "I have the details you provided as well as headlines I pulled up on the Net. I'll reach out to my contacts."

Linc cleared his throat of the emotion clogged there. "Appreciate it."

He closed his cell and tossed it onto the bed. He'd been here thirty-some-odd hours and he had already hit a brick wall. Every part of him believed this woman was Lori. Yet he had no way to prove it.

He closed his eyes and allowed the memories to invade his mind. Lori had come to the LAPD straight from college. Linc had just made detective. They were married within three months. A year later she was on the narco team with him. They'd been assigned to the Marcos operation because they fit the necessary profile—young and attractive. Marcos surrounded himself with youth and beauty. It was the only way into his exclusive, lethal club.

Just nine weeks later Linc and Lori had moved into the inner sanctum. Many weeks later, a celebration on the Marcos yacht was the prelude to his takedown. All his major players were to be there. But a competitor had seized the opportunity to take out all the real competition in one fell swoop.

It had worked.

Agony swelled inside Linc. He'd lost her and nothing else had mattered since.

He reached for his phone. Might as well walk around town and see what he could dig up in the way of info on Mia Grant. Hanging around the town's only hotel, an ancient house that had been converted into a bed-and-breakfast, would have him climbing the walls.

He stuffed his shirt back into his jeans and left. Downstairs the lady who'd registered him as a guest looked up from the paperback book she was reading and smiled. She hadn't been at her desk when he'd returned half an hour ago.

"Good afternoon, Mr. Reece. Did you have lunch? I can warm you up a plate. Our guests are welcome to all meals prepared."

"Thanks, but I'm on my way out." He flashed her a halfhearted smile.

"I hear you're going to buy the Reid house."

The small-town grapevine was obviously alive and well. "I'm considering it." He continued toward the door. Adding to the rumor mill wasn't on his agenda. Slowing for additional conversation would lead to questions he didn't want to answer.

"Mia will make that place look like the day it was built." Her face gleamed with pride. "She's just amazing."

Linc changed course and headed for the desk where the chatty lady sat. Either she was guessing or Mia had already discussed taking the job with someone on the gossip loop. "Are her prices reasonable?" Seemed like a safe lead-in.

"Never heard nobody complain." She pursed her lips and lifted her chin triumphantly.

"Mrs. Crist, you sound like a big fan of Miss Grant's. I'm not sure you're objective." Mrs. Crist, the owner of the bed-and-breakfast, was seventy if she was a day, but her eyes were as keen as a seventeen-year-old's.

"I'm a fan rightly enough," she confessed. "But the girl's got a magic touch with plaster. That's the God's truth."

"Do she and her husband work together?"

Mrs. Crist puckered her face with a combination of humor and confusion. "Where in the world did you hear she had a husband?" Her gaze narrowed. "You been talking to that Teddy Stewart down at the Gas and Go? That young fella is just trying to ward off any suitors. Mia's not married. She doesn't even have a boyfriend. She's too busy for such." She raised her eyebrows at Linc. "Or so she says."

Linc chuckled. "If we come to an agreeable price, I plan to keep her busy for a while."

Crist grinned. "I see she's already turned your head."

His tone as he'd made the statement reverberated in his ears, then kicked him square between the eyes. He'd sounded exactly like a man interested in more than a woman's professional skills. Not a good thing. He needed time with Mia Grant, not to scare her off. He needed to be sure.

"Only for her talent with plaster." He gave the lady a nod and headed for the door before he stuck his foot any deeper down his throat.

Outside he rounded the corner of the Victorian bed-and-breakfast and reached for his keys. He'd considered using an alias while he was here, but he wanted Mia to know his name. To hear it. To say it.

Linc wanted whoever had brought her here to know he had arrived. He was here for his wife.

His cell vibrated.

He hit the remote and unlocked the SUV as he tugged the phone from his pocket.

Unknown number with a Tennessee area code. Tension rushed through his veins, escalating his already too-fast respiration. "Reece."

"Mr. Reece, this is Mia Grant."

"You found time in your schedule?" He held his breath in anticipation of her answer.

"Yes."

The air seeped from his lungs.

"I'd like to meet at the house and see what you have in mind."

The sound of her voice made his knees rubbery. "Name the time." Damn. They needed to include the real estate agent. He'd have to call her immediately. The sooner he could see this Mia Grant again the sooner he would find the answers he needed.

"I'll pick up the key from Chandra and meet you there in fifteen minutes," she said.

Even better. "I'll be there."

She said goodbye and ended the call.

Linc leaned against his SUV and closed his eyes. Her voice...Lori's voice.

His wife was alive.

Chapter Four

The house looked as bad as Mia remembered. The plaster was a real mess, more the walls than the molding. The ceilings had some bad areas, but fortunately the original wood floors were in considerably better condition. The windows and doors looked salvageable. Surprisingly, the two baths and the kitchen were in better condition than any other room, which was good considering they could suck up major bucks in a renovation.

"I can work with this," she announced.

Reece nodded. "When can you start?"

Mia laughed. "Don't you want to know my price first?" He'd followed her from room to room for the last half hour. He hadn't said a word since the initial hello.

Surprise flashed across his face, but he quickly schooled the expression. "Mrs. Crist tells me your prices are fair."

"Maybe so." Mia didn't know this man. She wanted no miscommunications between them. "But I'd feel more comfortable if we agreed upon a price first."

He nodded his head. "Understandable."

Mia chewed the inside of her cheek. Perhaps the price she'd mentally calculated was too low. No, it was fair. She wouldn't jack up her price simply because he appeared prepared to pay whatever she named. This man was from out of town and clearly money was no issue, that was true. Still, right was right. She stated her price and prepared for his reaction.

"Sounds reasonable," Reece said without hesitation or detectable reluctance.

"It'll take some time," she warned. "I have a couple of days left at the Dowe house." Day and a half maybe. Better to give herself sufficient time than to risk not meeting a stated target date. "I'll need at least two weeks here."

Some aspect of her answer didn't appear to sit well with him. A frown furrowed his brow. "Is it possible to work a couple of hours here each day while you finish up there?"

A frown of her own worried her forehead. "Are you on a deadline, Mr. Reece?"

"Linc."

"Linc," she echoed. His stare turned so intense that she suddenly felt uncomfortable alone with him.

Knock it off, Mia. She squared her shoulders against the uneasiness. "You should call me Mia."

"Mia."

Silence thickened in the room as her senses absorbed the sound of her name on his lips. What was it about this man that made her feel so...restless?

"You...you have a deadline?" He hadn't answered her question.

He crossed the parlor to the expanse of windows looking out over the well-manicured lawn. The city council required that properties in town, whether inhabited or not, be maintained on the outside. Overgrown and littered yards were bad for tourism as well as community pride.

"Time isn't an issue," he said, his back still turned to her. "I'm merely anxious to get started."

That was true of most folks when they got their hearts set on a project. "I could maybe get a couple hours in tomorrow afternoon. I'll pick up enough material to get started."

He nodded. She noticed only because she was watching for a response. Her initial analysis of him had been right. Brooding. "Okay, then. See you tomorrow." Tucking her notepad into her apron pocket, she started for the entry hall.

"Are you available for dinner this evening?"

Startled by the request, Mia paused. He was watching her. That was it, she realized. He didn't really look at her. He watched her. Analyzed her. And it made her restless. "Dinner?"

"I'd like to discuss any recommendations you might have for the other work."

She nodded. "Plumbing and electrical. And the floors."

"Is that a yes to dinner?"

He moved closer, his posture oddly rigid. That restlessness she'd been experiencing picked up its pace, making her pulse quicken. Was he trying to intimidate her or was this just his way?

"Blossom Café?" she proposed. It was a safe choice. She knew the folks who ran the café and she would know all the patrons. Her little bungalow was only a couple of blocks away. It was perfect.

"Eight?"

He was definitely from the city, she thought. "Around here we call it supper and it's around six."

Why did he stare at her that way? Every response came after a considerable delay.

"Six, then."

More of that breath-stealing silence followed.

Suppressing that danged uneasiness, she tacked a smile into place. "See you then."

Mia turned toward her original destination. This time he didn't stop her. She walked out the door and straight to her old truck. The safety and familiarity of it felt like a balm to her frayed nerves. More than forty years old and a little beat-up, the truck served her purposes just fine. A handy toolbox was mounted in the back and a smaller, handheld version waited in the cab. She liked her truck and she liked her life.

Feeling out of sorts wasn't the norm for her, at least not in a really long time. Back during her recovery there had been a lot of days filled with pain and uncertainty. Feelings of loss that she hadn't been able to fully measure or articulate. But those days were long gone.

As Mia slid behind the wheel of her trusty truck she caught a glimpse of Mr. Reece watching her from the broad parlor window.

Doubt slipped up on her. Maybe she'd made a mistake agreeing to work for him. There was something very odd about Lincoln Reece. He exhumed frailties she hadn't suffered in years.

Mia shook her head. *You're making too much of this, girl.* She laughed. This was Blossom. Bad things never happened here. That was just another reason why she loved it so very much. It was also why her uncle had brought her here after her release from those long, long months of rehabilitation.

This was home now.

Safe. Reliable. Calm.

LINC COULDN'T MOVE.

He'd made that mistake when he'd asked her about

dinner. The closer he'd gotten to her the more his control had dwindled. He'd wanted to grab her and shake her. To demand that she admit that Mia Grant was not her name.

She was Lori...his wife.

Relief, elation and anticipation infused his blood with yearning. He felt it all the way to the core of his being.

The junker of a pickup eased away from the curb. When it had disappeared down the tree-lined street, Linc left the window and surveyed the parlor. There was a lot of work to be done. That would buy him some time. But there were other pressing issues to be considered.

How had Lori gotten here?

Who had rescued her after the explosion on the yacht? More importantly, how had she been rescued? Not that Linc wasn't grateful, but this was no act of a Good Samaritan. Her rescue had sinister origins. Otherwise her identity would have been tracked down and her next of kin—her husband—contacted.

As right as finding her felt, the circumstances were wrong, way wrong.

Blossom Café, 6:00 p.m.

SHE WAITED AT A TABLE in the center of the small café. For a minute or so Linc studied her. He'd already done a lot of that. It wasn't smart to risk her catching him yet again. He sensed she was suspicious already, but he couldn't help himself. From a distance, he could look with the knowledge that this was his wife. The only woman he had ever loved. The woman with whom he had shared every aspect of his life. Back when he'd had a life.

Seven years. At first he had plunged into an oblivion of pain and despair. He had prayed his way back, believing that there had to be a mistake...that she had to be alive. All he had to do was find her. Then defeat had conquered him and he had stopped feeling at all. Inside, he had broken. Given up.

Yet, there she was. The minimal outside changes didn't matter. It was the inside, the voice, the mannerisms that told him his heart could dare to beat again.

This was his wife and she was alive.

Linc pulled open the door, causing the overhead bell to jingle, and stepped inside. The smell of home cooking made the air thick and damp. Though clearly deep in conversation, most of the patrons glanced his way. Some turned back to their supper companions while others visually followed him to Lori's table. Mia's table. He had to remember that.

A smile stretched her lips—lips he had kissed a thousand times. "Did you have trouble finding the place?" The twinkle in her eyes told him she understood that was impossible since this was the only café on the town square open past three in the afternoon.

"I was delayed by a call." He dragged out the chair opposite her and took a seat.

She passed him a menu. "I already know what I want. The meatloaf is awesome."

He didn't bother looking at the menu. "Meatloaf it is, then."

"Good call." She held up her glass. "Sweet tea?"

What he really needed was a fifth of bourbon. "Absolutely."

Linc was vaguely aware that a waitress had strolled up to their table, but he couldn't shift his focus from the eyes, the mouth he'd cherished for a few short months and then had hungered for during the better part of a decade that had felt more like an eternity.

Mia placed their orders. When the chatty waitress had moved away, Mia pulled out her notepad. "I have a couple of names for you. Jesse Steele is the best plumber anywhere around here." She pointed to the next name she'd jotted down. "Same goes for Patrick Nunley. He's an electrician." She tapped the final name on her handwritten list. "I've worked with Jerry Brooks plenty of times. He's the best carpenter I know. He can handle anything else you need."

That her lips had stopped moving told him she was waiting for a response from him.

"I'll need estimates." He gave himself a mental kick. He needed to focus.

"I can have these guys call you," she suggested. "Or when I'm at the house they can come by and do their estimates."

"Either way works for me." He wanted to get past talk of the house.

"I'll make the calls." She tore the page free of the pad and thrust it at him. "You can keep this, so you don't forget the names."

He accepted the list and studied the names written there. A knot formed in his chest. This was not her handwriting. The *J*'s were different. And the way she crossed her *J*'s. Too neat, not the sweeping strokes Lori had made.

"Here you go." The waitress placed their orders on the table, heaping plates, then filled-to-the-rim glasses garnished with lemon wedges. "Anything else?"

Mia looked to him. Still in a daze of harsh reality, Linc shook his head.

"That's good for now, Louise. Thanks," Mia said.

She smiled that broad, familiar smile that was all Lori as she dismissed the waitress. The scent of buttered potatoes and richly seasoned meat turned his stomach. Linc had no appetite, despite the fact that he couldn't remember when he'd eaten last. Fear climbed up his dry throat and coagulated. What if he was wrong?

"Mmm." Mia closed her eyes as she savored a bite of meatloaf.

The question he'd intended to ask to shift the conversation stuck on the tip of his tongue, but he couldn't manage to spit it out. Not with his throat clogged with something he couldn't name and her making those sounds.

"You have to taste this." She gestured to his plate. "Eat!"

He wrapped his fingers around the fork, his movements mechanical, and followed her order. Whatever kept her here and talking to him. That was all that mattered...until he knew for sure. He ate a forkful. "You're right. The best I've ever tasted." An old memory slammed into his brain. "Except maybe that little place in Encino." He and Lori had eaten there several times because she had loved the down-home atmosphere. How had he forgotten that? "They served a pretty amazing meatloaf." He couldn't remember if they did or not, but they had served Southern-style cuisine.

She blinked. For one second he was certain she remembered. Then she said, "Encino? Is that where you're from?"

Another wave of defeat slammed into him. "L.A." He carefully placed the fork on the table. "My wife and I used to go to a little place in Encino. She loved the meatloaf." An ache broke open his chest. There was no trace of recognition on her face or in her eyes.

"You're married?" She looked surprised. Or was she disappointed?

He shook his head. "She died a long time ago."

Her face fell. "I'm sorry." She set her fork aside. "I shouldn't have asked, but it's unusual for a wife not to be involved with purchasing and remodeling a house. That's why I was surprised when you mentioned a wife." Her cheeks were a little pink. She'd always blushed like that whenever she felt she'd said the wrong thing.

"Sure." He swallowed back the disappointment that she had a logical reason for asking if he was married. Doubt and defeat were battling it out for top billing in his brain. The handwriting was wrong... the smile was right... Could she possibly be Lori or was he kidding himself? He'd given up hope a damned long time ago. How had it taken root again so deeply and swiftly?

Ten seconds turned into twenty. She picked at her meatloaf as if she were at a loss for words. He would have the advantage now. A change of subject would be a relief. He blanked his mind of those churning emotions he hadn't felt in so long. "Did you grow up in Blossom?"

Her gaze met his. "No. I'm from Colorado. I moved here about six years ago."

"You have family here?" He stopped breathing.

"My aunt." She chewed on another bite of her entrée. "My uncle visits often but he doesn't live here."

That was totally impossible. He bit the words back. Lori couldn't have family here. She had no living relatives anywhere. She'd been born and raised in California. Her parents had both been Californians. She had never spoken of any other relatives. After the accident, he'd attempted to track down any distant relatives, but there were none.

"Where did you learn about plasterwork?" He couldn't wait to hear the answer to that one. The fury that abruptly lit in his gut was irrational. He shouldn't feel any of this.

She laughed. "That's kind of a funny story." She sipped her tea, then licked her lips. "My aunt wanted to repair a hole in the plaster wall of her home. A plumbing repair had left a bit of a mess. I attempted to help her." She shrugged. "I figured it couldn't be that hard. I made the mess worse. But I wouldn't give up. After a while it was like I was a natural at it. Like I'd been an artisan of plaster in another life."

Because she had been. "And you've been doing it ever since?"

She nodded. "When I'm not helping out at the Pet Stop."

"Pet Stop?" He surely misunderstood her meaning.

"I help my aunt with her dog-grooming business. She's getting up there in years and she just can't keep up. I go over a couple of afternoons a week and lend a hand." Her lips curled into that crooked but sexy-as-hell grin that was all Lori. "But I don't mind. I love dogs. I'd have one of my own if I was ever home." She shrugged. "Maybe one of these days."

Her words hit him like a sucker punch to his gut. Could he be that wrong?

The voice, the eyes, the way she moved… He had been certain she was Lori.

But his wife had been seriously allergic to cats and dogs. She couldn't even live in an apartment where pets had lived before her.

His gaze fixed on the eyes and the lips that he knew so intimately and that had helped to convince him that this woman was his wife.

He should have known the whole concept of Lori being alive was too good to be true.

He'd made a mistake coming here.

Chapter Five

"It's him."

"You're certain?"

Ted Stewart checked the screen of his smartphone a third time, then glanced across the room to the table where Mia sat with the stranger who'd been hanging around watching her for two days. "I'm certain," he muttered under his breath. "And I checked the register at the bed-and-breakfast. It's him. Lincoln Reece."

Ted kept an eye on Mia as the man on the other line silently contemplated the news. This stranger was trouble. Ted couldn't ever recall Mr. Lopez calling three times in twenty-four hours about a situation involving Mia. He watched out for that girl as if she were his own daughter. Of course, she was his goddaughter. She called him her uncle but he wasn't really. He'd made a promise to his best friend on his deathbed that he would see that she was protected and cared for the rest of her life.

In Ted's opinion, Lopez went a little overboard. Even a straight-up guy like Ted couldn't get close to Mia. Old man Lopez guarded her like she was some kind of saint that no mere mortal was allowed to go near, much less touch.

"Keep an eye on him," Lopez ordered, dragging Ted back to the here and now. "I'm out of the country and I won't be able to get there for a few days. I want to know every move he makes."

Ted gave Reece a long, thorough look, something else he'd already done several times. "Who is this guy?" Ted asked quietly. The hum of conversation was plenty loud enough to cover his voice but he wasn't taking any chances. One of these days, if Ted had his way, Mia would belong to him. In small towns like Blossom a guy had to stake his claim early on. Most men his age moved to Nashville or Murfreesboro for better jobs. Not many stayed in this one-horse town where fabrication and industry were frowned upon. *Green* and *all-natural* were the only buzzwords these folks understood.

"An old enemy of Mia's father. He must be watched closely."

"Is this dude dangerous?" Apprehension nudged Ted. He'd never carried a pistol. He owned a shotgun but it hung on the rack inside his truck. Other than the time he'd had to run off that coyote, the rack was where the shotgun stayed.

"Suffice it to say, he's potential trouble."

"All right." Teddy tossed back a swig of his iced tea. "I'll keep an eye on him." He could use the extra bucks. Lopez always paid well. Not to mention he liked that the old man trusted him. Besides, spending time watching Mia was no hardship, and Ted had a feeling that keeping up with Reece's comings and goings would probably include seeing a lot of Mia.

"Do not underestimate Reece," Lopez warned. "He is not your average Joe."

Enough already. "Got it. I'll use extra caution."

"Contact me if anything changes." With that, Lopez severed the connection.

Ted tucked the phone into his pocket and dug into his supper. The gravy on his chicken-fried steak had turned cold but he wasn't wasting good money or good food. It ticked him off that Lopez had harped on just how special Reece was. Lopez should know by now that Ted knew how to handle himself. This wasn't the first time he'd taken care of unwanted attention on Mia's behalf.

He could handle this. Easy as the cherry pie he was going to have for dessert.

Lincoln Reece had better watch himself.

Chapter Six

Chicago, 6:30 p.m.

Slade Keaton relaxed at his usual table at the coffee shop. Maggie, the owner, had learned long ago to reserve this table for him. It was the perfect spot. For months he had been coming here around three-thirty or so each weekday afternoon so that he could watch the comings and goings across the street.

The Colby Agency. Practically a landmark in Chicago and one of the most renowned private investigations agencies in the country. Owned and operated by Victoria Colby-Camp and her son Jim, the agency's top-notch staff worked more like a family than a group of colleagues. One magazine had recently named the agency a model by which all others should conduct business.

Slade studied the fourth-floor windows, most of which were dark now. Only a handful of employees remained at this hour. Victoria and Jim, of course. Simon Ruhl and Ian Michaels, the agency's seconds-in-command. And the infamous Lucas Camp, Victoria's husband.

Anger simmered deep inside Slade. Would the proud and esteemed Victoria Colby have married the man had she known what Slade knew? Lucas had blinded her with stories of his heroic deeds, like saving the life of her first husband when he was a prisoner of war, Jim's father. She thought she knew Lucas. His lifetime as a career spook with the CIA assured that the better part of his history was top secret. But Slade knew many of his deepest, darkest secrets. And Victoria actually knew things that would help put together the final pieces. She had no idea how damaging those fragments were.

Lucas Camp was going to fall. Slade intended to see to it, if it was his last act before dying. He had prepared well. For years he had searched and pieced together information by whatever means necessary. Slowly but surely he had assembled his case just like a good attorney. Once he'd accomplished that step, he had positioned himself strategically. He'd purchased the Equalizer firm from Jim Colby, hired a staff and waited for an opportunity.

That opportunity had presented itself a short time ago, when one of Lucas's old enemies—and he had many—had made an attempt at vengeance using

Victoria. Because Slade had contacts in the murky world of intelligence he had gotten tipped off to the threat ahead of Camp. Slade watched Victoria and her son so closely that he had been in the perfect position to step in. He was now a friend of the family, though one of whom they remained wary.

A rare smile lifted the corners of Slade's mouth. Months of watching and waiting had finally paid off.

The next step in Slade's plan was the final and easiest of all. Systematically take Lucas Camp's perfect life apart.

"Would you like more coffee, sir?"

Slade looked up at the woman who had spoken. Maggie. Sweet, beautiful Maggie. She smiled, the expression full of promise for later. This was her coffee shop. He had needed visual access to the Colby Agency, and this coffee shop had provided it. Getting cozy with the owner had been the simplest way to hold the position. The fact that the people at the Colby Agency thought so highly of her was an unexpected perk.

"Definitely." Slade waited until she had filled his cup. "We have a very special invitation for the Fourth. You should mark your calendar."

Her eyes lit with anticipation. "Does it have anything to do with passports?"

"Afraid not."

Her expression fell. Maggie had been dreaming of taking a trip to Ireland and tracking down her ancestors. It still surprised him that she could believe he was the man with whom she could plan a future. Oh, well. Collateral damage was inevitable.

Maggie propped her smile back into place. "Don't keep me in suspense."

"We've been invited to the Colby Agency's Fourth of July celebration."

Disappointment flared briefly in her eyes. "That's very nice of Victoria and Lucas to include us."

"It is." It was the pivotal step Slade had been waiting for.

An employee called out to Maggie and she excused herself. Slade turned back to the view across the street. He had no place he needed to be tonight. His source had already reported in. Slade would pass along the details of the report as soon as Reece checked in. He knew how anxious Reece was for an update, but Slade needed to give him this information personally. No text message or email. This could prove too dangerous for Reece, under the circumstances.

Reece wasn't going to like what Slade had learned. Whatever Lincoln Reece had thought he'd known, he had been wrong.

Reece had a monumental decision to make. Let

the past go or attempt to unravel the mystery and perhaps die trying.

Then again, Slade had made that same decision two years ago.

And he wasn't dead yet.

Chapter Seven

Blossom, 8:01 p.m.

"You don't have to walk me home."

"If I don't, how will I know where you live?" Linc inhaled a chestful of fresh, country air—mostly to buy time to come up with a reasonable excuse for needing to know where she lived. There was no reason for her to know that he already had her address, date of birth and her social. "Just in case you try to run out on the job."

"I see." Mia's lips quirked into that smile that had haunted him for seven years. "I suppose you have a point. Not that I've ever run out on a job."

She walked slowly toward the cross-street to the right. He followed. Her home was no more than three blocks away. Up one and over a block or so more.

He liked watching the glow from the streetlamps dance on her dark hair. She'd let it down tonight.

Looking at the long, silky tresses made his fingers itch to tangle in them. The image of her dragging that lush mane over his bare skin lit a fire along that same path. He clenched his teeth.

"Why haven't you married again?"

The question came so far out of left field that he almost stumbled. His bum leg had been bugging the heck out of him. "I guess I never found closure." The truth seemed the best avenue to take.

She checked the quiet streets before taking a right at the intersection of Maple and Cedar, then she glanced up at him. "It's hard. Especially if the loss is sudden."

He didn't mind her questions, they gave him a legitimate reason to ask more of his own. "Sudden. Yes." She'd always been so full of life, so seemingly unstoppable, losing her that way had been the last thing he'd expected. He'd expected they would grow old together, like Mort and his wife.

"Car crash?"

Linc was surprised that she had so many questions. She'd seemed reluctant to ask the hard ones earlier. Not that he minded. "They say she died in an explosion."

Pausing, she frowned at him. "They say?"

"Yeah." The hair on the back of Linc's neck stood on end. He resisted the impulse to look behind them. Someone was watching. He could feel it as surely as he felt the faint breeze whispering across his bare arms. "Her body was never found." He shrugged. "I guess I can't accept that she's dead without a body."

"That's terrible." She stopped and stared up at him. "When did this happen?"

He wished she hadn't stopped midway between streetlamps. The ability to see the expression in her eyes would have been helpful. He took another deep breath, using the few seconds to look around. A shadow disappeared behind a truck parked at the curb, maybe half a block back. Yes, they were definitely being followed. "Seven years ago."

"I guess there's no expiration date on hope." She started forward again. "Or grief, for that matter." She said the last with a lingering sideways look at him.

Pain seared through him—a pain that had nothing to do with his beat-up right leg. "I turned all that off a long time ago."

"You're not running away?" This time her gaze collided with his beneath a streetlamp and he didn't miss the worry there.

He laughed, a little more drily than he'd meant to. "I don't run, Miss Grant." Right. He'd been running for five years. But she didn't need to know that.

"Why here?" She stopped again, this time at the sidewalk that led to her door. "You have distant relatives in the area?"

"No relatives. I was just passing through and this seemed as good a place as any to buy a second home."

"One far away from city life?" Her eyes twinkled with mischief.

"Very far away." Right now, right here, Linc wanted to kiss her. To taste her, just to see if she tasted the same. But that would be a major strategic error.

She nodded and led the way to her door. Flowers lined the narrow walk. Two steps climbed to the stoop. She stopped there and turned to him, an unspoken warning that this was as far as he would be going tonight.

"I'll see you tomorrow afternoon." She held out her hand. "Ready to work."

Linc closed his right hand around hers. It was small, soft and warm. His soul reacted instantly, sending a new surge of pain straight to his heart.

"I look forward to getting started." His voice cracked a little. He released her, lowering his hand to his side. The abrupt disconnect locked his jaw in simmering frustration.

Turning his back and walking away was hard as hell. He wanted to shake her. To demand answers. To make her see. But he couldn't be sure yet.

He couldn't be sure of anything, particularly his sanity.

"Good night," she called out.

He didn't look back, just waved as he strode away. Looking back would have shattered his already crumbling resolve.

An entire block had disappeared behind him before he pulled himself together enough to raise an internal alert for the shadow that had been tailing them. The tail had either backed off or had decided he'd seen all he needed to see.

His cell vibrated, so he snagged it from his pocket. "Reece."

"Word is that Grant's uncle, Vincent Lopez, is a major South American businessman who took over the family farm in Blossom to honor his long-deceased ancestors after his brother died. He owns a large property, family mansion included, just outside the town limits."

Slade Keaton. Linc had been waiting for his call. This news was not really news. This was exactly what he'd been expecting and he damned sure didn't believe in coincidences. Marcos had been born in Mexico City, but he'd later become an American citizen. This so-called uncle just happened to be Latino, too? No way. "You get a visual of this guy?"

"I'm working on it," Keaton assured him. "The thing is, if this Lopez is Marcos, and Grant is...your wife, how did they survive without assistance? This didn't happen without big-time connections on both sides."

Did he think Linc didn't get that part? He bit back the antagonism. "What about the hospital where she was treated?"

"I can tell you right now," Keaton guaranteed, "it wasn't in this country unless it was a private facility way off the radar. I'll find it. Don't sweat that one. I won't stop nudging contacts until I do."

"I need a visual on Lopez," Linc reminded his boss. "The sooner, the better."

Only after Linc ended the call did he realize he hadn't even thanked Keaton. He should have. This wasn't business. This was personal.

The possibility that someone inside LAPD had passed information to Marcos or somehow assisted him twisted deep in Linc's gut. He opened his cell and entered a number he hadn't reached out to in five years, yet still knew by heart.

"Hello."

It was a woman's voice, high-pitched but shaky. Mort's wife. For a moment Linc worried it was too late to call, but L.A. was two hours behind central Tennessee. "Iris, this is Linc. Is Mort handy?"

There was an extended silence, then a rustling sound. "Hello, this is Megan. Who's this?"

Mort's daughter. "Megan, this is Lincoln Reece. Mort and I used to be partners." Megan had been a wild teenager back then; she might not remember Linc.

"Mr. Reece, I remember. Just a moment."

He heard a verbal exchange, too muffled to make out, then another round of silence. Finally, Megan continued, "I'm sorry, but I needed to go to another room. I don't want to talk about this in front of Mother."

Linc's instincts roared a warning. "What's going on?"

"My father..."

Linc's insides went deathly still.

"He and Mother returned home on Saturday afternoon. That night, after Mother had gone to bed, he went out to the garage and...shot himself."

Shock quaked through Linc. A band of tangled emotions tightened around his chest. "I don't understand. I just spoke to him on Friday night. I thought he and Iris were on a road trip." This made no sense at all. Had they driven all night to reach L.A. after the stop in Chicago? Why the hell would Mort do that? He had finally retired.

"We don't know what happened." She exhaled a shaky breath. "He didn't leave a note."

"He didn't mention anything to anyone?" Mort was a man who could keep a secret for as long as necessary. That was true. Thirty years in undercover work ensured that deeply ingrained trait.

"It's…just unbelievable. We're all in shock. Mother said that after their trip to Tennessee he was extremely quiet. She couldn't get him to talk about whatever was bothering him."

"He mentioned that your mother had always wanted to visit Nashville." Linc hadn't picked up on any troubling vibes…other than Mort's insistence that Lori was alive and living here in Blossom.

"That's strange. He was the one who insisted on the trip to Tennessee," Megan said. "The only part of Nashville they saw was the airport. Mother said he rented a car and they drove straight to some little town. They stayed overnight, flew to Chicago, then home. Something in that little town upset him, but he wouldn't talk about it at all."

Wait. That was wrong. "The trip to Blossom, Tennessee was Mort's idea?" She'd just said as much but Linc had to be sure. "Iris didn't suggest the trip as part of a cross-country getaway?"

"Mother had never heard of the place. With her arthritis getting worse, traveling was too difficult but she didn't want him to make this trip alone. She had no idea that the reason he insisted on stopping in Chicago was to see you until they were home. He just told her he had something he had to do. After he…his death we couldn't call you. We didn't have the number."

A cold, ruthless knot planted itself deep in Linc's

throat. He tried to clear it away and failed miserably. "I...I don't know what to say. Mort seemed the same old Mort when we talked." This was crazy. "Is there anything I can do?" It wasn't much of an offer, but it was the best he could do.

"Thank you, Mr. Reece, but there's nothing anyone can do now. He's gone and I doubt we'll ever know why he chose to leave us this way."

Struggling to hold it together, Linc promised to keep in touch and ended the call.

He stood there in the dark for a long while. Moving was out of the question. Mort was dead. He had killed himself. After discovering the woman here in Blossom, Mia Grant. After giving that news to Linc.

No, wait. Something was way off. How had Mort known to come to Blossom? If coming here wasn't his wife's idea, he had to have had a reason for picking this small, out-of-the-way town.

But the bigger question was why he lied to Linc about any of it. Why not just spell it all out?

Why seek him out and lie about how he'd discovered the woman he suspected was Lori? None of it made any kind of sense. Blossom wasn't a major tourist attraction, and Mort sure as hell wasn't a plant lover. He had paid a neighbor's kid to mow his lawn.

There was no logical reason for him to have come here.

Unless he'd known she was here.

Linc's bum leg gave out, throwing him off balance. He grabbed back his equilibrium and sucked in a breath. No way.

No way.

There had to be another explanation.

Bile roiling in his gut, Linc forced one foot in front of the other. The bed-and-breakfast was his destination. He needed a drink. He hadn't let a single drop pass his lips since laying eyes on her.

But right now, it might be the only way he survived the night without doing something stupid.

Like tearing this whole damned town apart for some answers.

Chapter Eight

Tuesday, June 28, 2:10 p.m.

Mia scooted out of her truck and hurried up the walk to her aunt's nineteenth-century antebellum house. The call for an impromptu visit had been worrying Mia for the past hour, but her aunt had insisted that she should wait until she was finished for the day before coming by.

They needed to talk.

Mia and her aunt visited frequently, but this felt different. Her aunt had sounded unnerved. Almost nothing rattled Gloria Lopez. She worked with animals every day, not to mention their sometimes neglectful masters, and she never ran out of patience. If something was bothering Gloria, it was a pretty big deal.

"Gloria?" Mia called as she poked her head inside the front door. Most folks, especially family, didn't bother to knock when dropping by. Mia usually did knock but she was expected so the formalities weren't necessary. Besides, Gloria had customers in and out most days.

"In here, Butterfly!"

Mia found her aunt in the big back room she'd transformed into her pet oasis. She did the grooming on an enclosed back porch, but this room was designed, decorated and lovingly used as a haven for her four-legged customers. Gloria sat in a big old rocker swaying back and forth with a beagle in her lap.

"She's been upset since her mommy dropped her off an hour ago." Gloria rubbed the dog between the ears. "But she's just about ready for her bath."

Plopping into a matching rocker, Mia smiled. The pets Gloria groomed were very lucky animals. A couple of Labs were sprawled on the floor. Neither one bothered to lift his head at Mia's arrival, though they swished their tails. Three cats were curled up on window ledges or the backs of chairs.

Gloria Lopez was an amazing woman who had turned her widowhood into a beautiful thing. She swore that she just couldn't think of a better way to spend Edward's insurance money. Mia had a feeling that Gloria used the animals to keep the loneliness at bay. Even ten years later Gloria couldn't see herself with anyone but Edward. Now that was love.

Not a day passed that Mia didn't wonder if she would ever know what that kind of love was like. The image of Lincoln Reece filtered through her brain. She banished it, wondering what in the world made her think of the man. "So what's up?"

Gloria pouched her lips into a pout. "What happened to *hello* and *how was your day?*" She shook her head, sending her store-bought, golden, curly locks tossing side to side. The pale color was a sharp contrast to her olive skin. Gloria had been born in Mexico but her Tennessee rearing had insured she spoke like a true Southern lady. Her only accent was the famous Dixie drawl. "You young people have no appreciation for the art of conversation."

"Sorry." They had this debate at least once a week. "How was your day?"

Gloria tipped her head around in a dramatic circle and widened her eyes. "Cra…zy. Katherine Ingle let Trixie get all matted then she burst into tears when she saw how short I had to trim the poor thing's coat. Dwayne Lester's grandpa passed and he had to leave Sheba and Shad with me." She hitched her head toward the two Labs. "He hasn't a clue when he'll be back." She blew out a big breath and eyed Mia knowingly. "Then your uncle Vince called all worked up."

Finally, they were getting to the reason for this command visit. "Is something wrong?"

"He's worried about you." Gloria settled the beagle on the rug. "Let's have a glass of tea."

Mia really needed to go. She still had to get over to the Reid house. Mr. Reece would be waiting. But trying to get away before her aunt was ready for her to go was next to impossible. Besides, ignoring her uncle's concerns usually prompted a visit where he would obsess over Mia's decisions and activities. The man was going to worry himself into an early grave. According to Gloria, her husband, Vince's brother, had been every bit as bad.

In the kitchen, Gloria poured two tall glasses of iced tea and settled them on the big table in the center of the room. "Vince is concerned that you're working too hard." Gloria gave her that knowing look again. "You know what the doctors said about that."

Here they went. "Aunt Gloria, I'm fine." The doctors had warned Mia about physical and mental stress when she'd first left the rehabilitation clinic. That had been almost six years ago. "It's been four years since I was officially released from medical care. I can be normal now." Mia said the last a little more pointedly than she'd intended. Gloria noticed.

"Your father would have wanted Vince and me to take good care of you. You were everything to him."

Mia felt instantly contrite. Gloria and Vince had

given up a great deal to take care of her. Those first two years had been rough. Mia had required round-the-clock care. She'd had dozens of surgeries. Relearning everything from walking to reading and writing had been necessary. That metamorphosis was why they had nicknamed her Butterfly. Mia owed them both a great deal. She couldn't imagine what would have become of her without them.

"I know, and I appreciate the concern. But I'm fine." Despite her best efforts, exasperation filtered into Mia's voice. "You know how Uncle Vince is. If he had his way I'd lie on the sofa all day with servants waiting on me hand and foot."

Gloria smothered a smile with a sip of tea. "You don't need to work so hard. Your father left you well cared for." She shook her head. "I don't see why you insist on taking on projects."

Now Mia got it. They'd heard about Lincoln Reece. Her uncle was insanely protective. The idea of Mia working for a stranger had likely sent him through the roof. "I love my work." A cat curled around her ankles, rubbing against her leg.

"Vince would like you to come down to Bogotá for a few days. You haven't taken a vacation in ages."

Mia had to leave. She wasn't going to get hijacked into this any deeper. She stood. "Gloria, I have an appointment. I have to go. I'll call Uncle Vince tonight.

Taking a vacation right now is out of the question. Maybe next month."

The trapped expression on her aunt's face warned that she was mentally scrambling for a logical counter. Before she could come up with something, Mia rounded the table and kissed her on top of the head. "I'll talk to you later. Tell Uncle Vince to stop worrying." Mia sighed. "I'm a grown, healthy woman. I can take care of myself."

"Just be careful," Gloria cautioned. "No one knows this man who just blew into town throwing money around. He might not be what he appears to be."

Mia knew it. She promised to keep that in mind, then hustled out of there before her aunt thought of some other advice or counsel. Between her and Vince, Mia was lucky to breathe on her own.

Blossom was small so the drive to the Reid house took only seven minutes. Reece was there. At least, his SUV was parked behind the house. That was the one drawback to these old houses in town, if there was off-street parking it was in the back. Mia parked at the curb and grabbed her toolbox. She'd come back to the truck for a ladder. Mercy, she hated being late.

The front door opened as she climbed the steps. Reece nodded. "You made it."

Mia mentally cringed. "Yes, I did." She wasn't

going to bore him with details of her overprotective family. Instead, she thrust the toolbox at him. "Take this and I'll get the ladder."

"How about you keep that and I'll get the ladder."

He didn't wait for her answer. He crossed the porch and descended the steps, brushing right past her. Mia's breath caught. She swallowed, shook herself. Whatever aftershave or cologne he wore seriously messed with her olfactory system. Each time he was close she felt as if she couldn't breathe deeply enough. Silly allergies. She hadn't stumbled upon many things that triggered a reaction, but when she did it was usually brutal. Occasionally dogs and cats prompted a reaction but not so often. Hopefully, her client's scent wouldn't become too much of a problem.

That was a far better excuse than the other one making her suddenly too warm in her well-worn jeans and comfortable work T-shirt. She shook her head and walked through the door he'd left open. Inside, unexpected odors replaced the sexy male scent playing havoc with her senses. The house smelled of wood and paint cleaners. Either Reece or Chandra had hired a cleaning team. The old house sparkled. Too bad Mia was just going to make a new mess. Hard as she tried, there was no way to avoid some sanding.

"Where do you plan to start?"

Mia turned to Reece. She wondered if the grimace he wore was about the limp she'd noticed. Getting through that meal last night without asking about it had been a real test of her willpower. She had considered a dozen ways to introduce the topic, like the fact that she had a few pins and metal plates herself. Nearly two years of therapy had allowed her to function normally but it had been a long, hard road. Lord knew last night she had lost control of her tongue on the subject of his wife. She just hadn't been able to stop. She'd had to know.

"I always like to start with the worst and work my way to the not so bad." Cleaning up the mess was more efficient that way. "Since the rooms upstairs don't need any major plasterwork, how about I start with the ceilings down here?" Ceilings made the worst mess and the repairs were usually the most involved. Leaks and wiring changes were the typical culprits. They made for fairly large holes in the plaster. She pointed to the dining room. "Kitchen's got the metal ceiling, so I'll move from the dining room forward to the parlors and entry hall."

"Sounds like a plan." He moved the ladder to the dining room and set it up beneath the worst of the cracks and the areas of missing plaster.

He favored his right leg beneath the weight of the ladder. It wasn't that heavy but clearly the additional strain was uncomfortable for Reece. Mia bit her lips together to hold back the questions.

"I stocked the kitchen with snacks and drinks. If there's something you prefer, just say the word." He looked from the ladder to her.

Mia grinned. This guy really was anxious to get this work done. Folks who didn't want their contractors leaving the property for meals or breaks always provided refreshments. "Perfect." She hoped he wasn't going to stand around watching. Having an audience when working on one of the tour homes was vastly different from having a homeowner stand around and watch her every move.

Only one thing to do. She gathered her tools and the plaster compound and went to work. To distract herself from his watchful gaze, she hummed. She knew better than to try singing. That would get her run off before she got the first coat skimmed on. Sadly, she could not carry a tune in a bucket.

Eventually Reece wandered from the room. Mia kept working, falling into that rhythm that was as familiar as breathing. The wider cracks required careful attention and numerous thin layers to bring the gaps level with the rest of the ceiling, more than a century old.

"Water?"

Mia blinked, drawing back from the intense focus of her work. "I'm sorry, what?"

He held out a bottle of water. "You've been working for more than an hour. I thought you might be thirsty."

Mia placed her pan and blade on top of the ladder and pulled a rag from her apron pocket to wipe her hands. "Sure." As she climbed down, a twinge nipped her left hip, making her wince. Reece was more right than he knew. A break was exactly what she needed. Staying on the ladder for too many hours in a day was a mistake she tried to avoid. But Reece had been anxious for her to begin and once she got going she lost all track of time.

"Thanks." She accepted the chilled bottle and twisted off the top. The cold water felt good sliding down her throat. She sighed with satisfaction. "I know it's not eco-smart but there's nothing handier than bottled water."

Reece was staring at her again. She should have gotten used to that by now. But this time he stared at her left hip.

"You take a tumble?"

There it was…her lead-in. Her curiosity was stirred. "Naw, it's an old injury."

He nodded, took a swig of his water.

"How about you?" She gestured to his leg.

"Old injury."

That hard-to-breathe sensation swooped in before she could fill her lungs. "Car accident seven years ago." She forced some more water down her suddenly tight throat. Her parents had died in that accident. Not a single memory of that night or the three months that followed had survived the brain damage she'd suffered. Her entire history had vanished from the scrambled gray matter in her skull.

"Boat explosion." He turned up the bottle, and the muscles of his throat flexed and contracted as he sucked down half the water. Then he rubbed the back of his hand across his mouth. "Seven years ago."

So, they had something in common. "Thirteen surgeries."

He raised his eyebrows. "Five."

"I lost my parents in the accident." Mia had no idea why she felt compelled to continue along these lines. She had the answer to why he favored his left leg. Somehow she felt totally comfortable talking about this with him, which was strange considering only a few moments ago she'd had difficulty breathing. Something he'd said before hit her hard. "Was this the same explosion…?"

He nodded. "Same one."

That choking sensation was back full force. "It's tough to go through something like that, especially when you lose your family in the same process."

"Yeah." He turned away, walked to the window. "One minute you have it all, the next minute it's gone."

He stood at the window, the jeans and shirt molded to a masculine body that looked anything but hollow or damaged. It looked so sexy, Mia had to tell herself to breathe. Why had he come here? He had no family or friends here. No wife or girlfriend to please. Why Blossom? That passing-through story was a cop-out. This place didn't fit her conclusions about him. He didn't fit anything about this town.

She dared to join him at the window. "You are running away." Last night he'd said he wasn't running.

"Some would call it that."

She studied his profile. The cut of his jawline. The high, lean cheekbones that lent a look of weariness and defeat to his somber words. The scar that spoke of tragedy. "What would you call it?"

He turned his face to hers and stared directly into her eyes. Her heart thumped hard. His eyes were such a vivid blue, they drew her, made her want to keep looking way past what was socially acceptable.

"I came here looking for something. I guess time will tell if I've found it."

That subtle scent he wore…his eyes…the sound of his voice. All of it bombarded her, prompting reactions she couldn't name. "I…" She licked her lips, which abruptly felt as parched as her throat despite the bottle of water. "I should get back to work."

"That song," he said, slowing her escape.

She turned back to him, her fingers tightening around the water bottle until it crinkled. "Song?"

"The one you were humming." He hummed a few notes in that deep, deep voice. She shivered as if a blast of winter air had swept through the old windows. "What's the name of it?"

Mia knew the one. It was old but she loved it. "'When a Man Loves a Woman.' Percy Sledge." That song was her favorite. She didn't remember where she'd first heard it.

He made a sound, not a laugh but something like that. "Thought so. It was my wife's favorite song. We danced to that song at our wedding."

Pain slashed through Mia's skull. She squeezed her eyes shut and waited for it to pass. Random pains went with the territory after surviving the kind of accident that claimed two other lives.

"You okay?"

She opened her eyes. He'd moved closer. Now he hovered so near that she couldn't draw in a breath without tasting his scent. "I'm good. Tired, that's all."

Mia walked deliberately to her ladder, fought back the crazy reactions he or his words had invoked and went back to work. She swiped her blade across the ceiling, worked hard at exiling him from her head. He stood right there in the middle of the room, watching her. His gaze was like a fire sweeping across her skin. She could feel the heat scorching every part of her that his eyes touched. *Ignore him. Don't look.*

She didn't relax until he left the room. Mia blew out a breath. This job was going to be a lot more complicated than she'd expected. "Not because of you," she muttered to the old house. It was *him*. He made her more uncomfortable than any person she could recall meeting.

The back door slammed hard, echoing through the empty house. Apparently she wasn't the only one who was uncomfortable. Maybe she'd asked too many questions. Another odd effect he had on her.

Mia worked for several more minutes until her curiosity got the better of her. Had he left? He hadn't come back into the house. She couldn't stand not knowing. If he came back in, she decided as she climbed down from her perch on the ladder, she would busy herself washing her hands in the kitchen sink. He would never know she'd been checking to see if he was still around.

The cleaning team had scrubbed the kitchen cabinets until they gleamed. They looked better than she'd expected. Add a new countertop and sink, maybe appliances, and the kitchen would be great. She peered out the big window over the sink.

Reece leaned against his SUV, his head back as if he were staring up into the trees. A frown inched its way across Mia's forehead. He'd said he was looking for something. Had he decided to start over far away from his old life? She had kind of done that, but the decision hadn't really been hers. Her aunt and uncle had made all the decisions for her. She couldn't actually complain. Mia hadn't been in any physical or mental condition to make the choices herself.

Maybe that was why she experienced such strong reactions to this stranger. Fate had dealt them both a pretty tough hand.

A crash in the dining room hauled her out of her amateur analysis. Breaking glass? She strode in that direction.

Broken glass glittered on the wood floor. Her gaze shifted from the floor to the windows that faced the side street. Jagged shards of glass outlined one of the wood sashes like bad teeth.

"What the...?" She surveyed the floor, looking for whatever had shattered the window. Her gaze landed on an electric hand sander. She stepped cautiously around the shards. Not just any hand sander. *Her* hand sander.

Someone had taken the small power tool from the toolbox in the back of her truck and thrown it through the window. In broad daylight.

"Why in the world...?"

She was at the door before she realized she had made the decision to go outside. Her truck sat right where she had left it. The toolbox was closed. Keys were still in the ignition. Mia never locked her truck, never removed the key. There had never been any reason to.

"You okay?"

Startled, she whipped around. Reece stood right behind her. The worry in his eyes surprised her almost as much as his catching her completely off guard. She hadn't heard a sound. For a guy with a limp that was saying something.

"I can't figure out what happened." She shrugged, shook her head. "Someone took my hand sander from my toolbox and threw it through your window." A historic window. Not so easily replaced.

Reece walked all the way around her truck, searched the interior and the toolbox. "Nothing was taken," she assured him. She didn't have that many power tools and the ones she had weren't top-of-the-line. Nothing but the truck itself had any real value and that was mainly to her. Still, it was bought and paid for.

Who would do this? She checked the street, considered the families who lived in either direction. There were kids but none who would do something like this.

"We should call Chief Taylor." What a way to welcome a new resident to town. "He'll file a report for your insurance." Jeez, what if Reece hadn't gotten insurance yet? She felt sick to her stomach. If he hadn't, she would pay for the damages.

"Don't worry about it." Reece, too, was surveying the street and the houses on either side of his. "Let's go back inside."

Mia dug in her pocket for her cell. "No, really, we have to call the chief."

Reece snagged her by the arm and hauled her toward his front door. "I said, don't worry about it."

By the time they reached the entry hall Mia had kicked aside the shock at his reaction and was barreling toward ticked off. "Wait." She dug in her heels. "I don't know how you do things in L.A. but here we report vandalism."

He didn't respond for the better part of a minute. His fingers still manacling her arm, he simply stared at her with those blue, blue eyes. "I don't want any unnecessary attention."

A new, startling revelation muscled its way into her brain, chasing away the burst of anger his manhandling had inspired. "Are you running from the law?" Good grief, she hadn't actually given any serious consideration to that possibility. This was Blossom. It was like Mayberry. Nothing bad ever happened here. Her throat tightened irrationally and her skin burned beneath his firm grip.

He shook his head. "I'm not running from anything." He released her and looked away. "I did that for five years. I won't run anymore."

Mia resisted the urge to follow him when he walked away. But every instinct she possessed wanted to help him find his way.

What was wrong with her? She didn't know this man yet she felt it was her responsibility to help him. To take care of him.

Maybe her uncle was right. Maybe she needed a vacation.

Mia rejected that idea. For too many of the past seven long years, doctors and physical therapists and family had been taking care of her, advising and guiding her. For the first time she felt as if she could do the helping. She had to try. For him and for her.

Chapter Nine

If he'd had any doubts about Mia Grant's true identity, Linc had none now.

His presence as well as his intent here was now known. The broken window was not vandalism. Blossom didn't have a reputation for trouble, not even the small stuff.

He had sensed that someone had followed him to her house last night after dinner. Now he knew for sure that he was being watched.

Linc rounded up the broom and dustpan the cleaners had left in the hall closet. He didn't have a trash can but the bags from his stop at the market would work. Grabbing a couple, he prepared to clean up the message someone had decided to send him.

"You need gloves for that." She backed toward the door. "I'll get a pair."

He opted not to say anything. He'd already said too much. Justification for not wanting to call the police wasn't going to be easily explained. It was a mistake he couldn't afford to repeat. Her story about how her parents had died in a car accident kept ringing in his ears. Lori's parents had died in a car crash when she was in college. He wasn't going to chalk that up to coincidence, even if he believed in the phenomenon.

Frustrated, he reached for a large shard of the windowpane, then another. He dropped them into the bag and reached for more.

"Here." She shoved the gloves at him. "Use these."

That she'd rushed back into the house without Linc noticing startled him. His fingers tensed, digging into the glass he'd forgotten he'd snatched up. Releasing the glass, he muttered a curse through clenched teeth.

"Oh, my word." She dropped the gloves. "I'll get the first aid kit."

Linc swore at himself all the way to the kitchen. He turned on the faucet and stuck his injured hand under the stream of cold water. He hissed another curse. Idiot! It had been a long time since he'd allowed emotions to distract him. Hell, he'd stopped feeling anything at all five years ago. It wasn't fair that it was so difficult to turn off his emotions while turning them back on happened almost instantly.

"Let me help you with that."

Linc jerked out his shirttail and dried his hand. Blood smeared, ruining the shirt. "Looks like I'm making matters worse."

She opened the kit and picked through the items inside. "Give me your hand." She held hers out palm up.

Linc didn't move; he simply stared at her hand. For seven years he had dreamed of touching her again. Not the brief handshake they'd shared when they first met, but of really touching her. He placed his hand in hers. The stinging in his fingers vanished. All he could feel was her soft, warm skin against his.

He watched as her delicate fingers, the same ones that wielded a plaster blade, gently dabbed the blood away.

"You're in luck." She looked up long enough to flash him a smile. "It's not deep enough for stitches." She turned her attention back to his hand. "Just deep enough to sting like hell and get in the way. A little antiseptic…" She applied the antibacterial salve from the tiny tube. "A little tight wrapping…" She encircled his hand in gauze. "And you'll be fine in a few days." She flashed that too-familiar smile for him again.

"Thanks." The impulse to grab her and run was overwhelming. But he couldn't do that. Not yet. He needed proof that she was his wife.

"I'll clean up." She gathered the items on the counter and repacked her first aid kit. Then she faced him. "I'll call it a day so you can take it easy."

She wanted out of here. As hard as she attempted to behave calmly Linc could feel the tension exuding from her. He needed to initiate some damage control.

"Before you go, I should explain."

That she hesitated gave him hope that he could fix this, but the apprehension in her eyes warned that it wouldn't be easy.

"There was a lot of publicity after the accident." He closed his eyes to block the memories that instantly slammed into him. "The press hounded me for months." He opened his eyes and met the uncertainty in her gaze with determination in his own. He could not screw this up. "I've been running away from that nightmare ever since." He shook his head. "I don't want to run anymore."

"I can't imagine." She set the kit back on the counter and swiped her hands on her apron. "We don't have to report this." A big breath hissed past her lips. "I'll ask around." She shrugged. "See if I can figure out who did something so mean."

Not a good idea. "Why don't we forget the whole thing? If," he added when the apprehension flickered in her eyes again, "there are any more incidents we'll call whoever you want." He turned his palms up, going for nonchalant. "Like you said, it was probably some kid acting out a dare. The sound of the glass breaking probably scared 'em to death."

She nodded. "Probably." Then she searched his eyes, concern still haunting hers. "If you're sure."

"I'm sure."

"Okay. I'll see you tomorrow then."

A new challenge jumped in front of him as she headed for the dining room. He needed more time with her. If what he suspected was true, he couldn't be sure of how much time he had. If Marcos was somehow still alive, he wouldn't wait long to make his move. Anticipating that move was simple. He would either attempt to get Linc out of the way or he would take *her* away.

Linc couldn't wait around for either one to happen.

Mia was already halfway to her truck with her toolbox before Linc grabbed the ladder and headed after her. She tossed her toolbox in the cab and then pulled her cell phone from her pocket. Linc listened as he loaded the ladder.

"I was going to call you after work. No. No. Really I was."

She seemed agitated at the caller.

"I can't do that right now."

Linc picked up bungee cords from the bed of

the truck and took his time securing the ladder. He wanted to listen as long as possible.

"I know you worry." She glanced at Linc but he kept his head down. "I'll call you tonight. I promise. Yes." She sighed. "Okay. Love you, too."

Linc fastened the final cord. It slipped and he winced as it slid through his hand.

"Family." She tucked the phone back into the pocket of her jeans. "They always think they know what's best for you."

"You think you won't miss that." He leaned against the truck. "Until you wake up one day and there's no one left but you."

She put her hand to her forehead. "I'm sorry. You're right. My uncle thinks I work too much."

"Do you?" Lori had been a total workaholic. Like him. They'd been the perfect pair.

"Maybe." She shook her head. "Isn't everyone's standard different?"

Lori would have argued her case with the same reasoning. His gut tightened. This was her. He was as certain of it as humanly possible. No matter that she no longer appeared to be allergic to dogs, Linc knew it was her. The idea that Mort may have been involved with whatever had gone down seven years ago thundered in his brain. Now Mort was dead and there was no way to know what he'd done or why he'd done it.

Linc had one chance here and he was looking right at her. "Good point." In an effort to buy some of that time he needed so badly, he said, "Did you mention having some paint chips that I could use for color selections?" She hadn't, but he was willing to bet she knew the handiest place to find color chips and paint. And he knew where he wanted her to find it.

That smile that turned him inside out spread across her lips. "You are anxious, aren't you?" She shot a look at the house. "It might be a few more days before you can paint."

"I think I'd like to go bold," he ventured.

"That's a big decision," she allowed, far more relaxed now.

"Agreed, but no more playing it safe for me. Maybe if I saw an older home like this painted in the richer colors, I could take the leap without hesitation." He was banking on the theory that she would want to help.

A moment passed as she considered his dilemma. "I could show you my uncle's house. He's away. He embraces all things bold."

Exactly what he'd hoped for. As soon as he'd gotten word from Keaton that Mia Grant had an uncle with a home here, he'd checked it out. At the crack of dawn this morning Linc had taken a look. Vincent Lopez did indeed embrace boldness, particularly in his interior design choices.

"Great." He waited, hoping.

She shrugged. "We could go now." Her gaze wandered to his hand. "If you want."

"Now is good." He had a feeling she felt bad about his injury and wanted to keep an eye on him for a little while.

"Climb in." She rounded the hood of her truck.

Linc pushed the toolbox to the center of the bench seat and dropped into the passenger side. He'd wangled more time.

What the hell did he do next?

Inspiration Lane, 5:15 p.m.

THE MANSION LOPEZ CALLED HOME whenever he was in Blossom was no typical farmhouse, not by a long shot. A number of words came to mind—*enormous, grandiose,* but definitely not *typical.* Juan Marcos had shown the same need for grandeur back in L.A. The county had auctioned off his assets after the explosion. Looked like he'd made his fortune back and then some.

Mia hit the light switch and quickly entered the security code. She turned to Linc and waved her arms. "This is as rich and bold as you can get."

"Interesting." Linc wandered through the entry

hall. He feigned admiration of the deep burgundy color and the massive paintings. The security system was high tech, the cameras the best on the market. If Lopez/Marcos were monitoring the system remotely, he would know someone had entered his home. He would see Linc. He stared directly at the nearest meticulously placed camera. If Marcos was behind this, Linc wanted him to know that he was here to reclaim what was his.

He indicated the massive room to the right. "May I see more?" She gave him the go-ahead with another sweep of her arms. Linc walked into the enormous parlor. She followed, turning on more lights.

More lavish decorating filled the space. Again, he checked out the distinction between the deep hues of the wall and the bright white wood detailing he'd checked out through the windows already. "I like the contrast." The occasional comment was necessary to avoid her suspicions.

"Most of the historic homes go that route. The vivid contrast helps to emphasize the detail work in the molding." She caressed the intricate door trim like a satiated lover.

His stomach tightened at the memory of her hands caressing his skin in just that way. He blinked away the distraction and moved to the ornate mantel. A barrage of framed photographs lined the marble top.

Linc's insides went as cold as the imported stone when his eyes lit on photos of Lori as a baby...her gap-toothed school photos...her high school graduation portrait... How in the hell had these ended up here? These were Lori's. For more than five years all her photos, all her things had been stored away under lock and key. No one had access...

No one except Mort. Linc had left a key to the climate-controlled storage unit with his mentor and friend. Betrayal twisted Linc's gut. He'd trusted Mort with his life, with Lori's life.

How much had Linc's relationship with Mort been worth? Linc's jaw tightened. He would never have believed Mort had a price. Not Mort. He had never skated even close to that line.

Another photo grabbed Linc by the throat. Lori with a man. A Latino. The nose and the chin were different, the head shaved, but it was him. Juan Marcos.

Emotion bombarded Linc. This was evidence. Circumstantial, maybe, but evidence that Mia Grant could be Lori Reece.

Linc faced the woman standing less than three feet away. His wife.

"My uncle." She shook her head. "He treats me like the daughter he never had."

Juan Marcos had no children. It was documented that he had a number of women he considered wives.

Two had been tracked down, only to discover they had died of suspicious causes. Linc hadn't confirmed his conclusion yet, but he figured this aunt Gloria was one of Marcos's female companions.

It was likely that Gloria's primary responsibility was to keep an eye on Mia...Lori.

"Your uncle clearly adores you." The bastard. Marcos was the kind of man who prided himself on taking what did not belong to him. "This is him?" He gestured to the photograph that had ice clogging his veins.

"That's him." She sighed, then shook her head. "He's far too protective." Her gaze traveled over the photographs. "Since the accident he treats me like I'm still this age." She pointed to the photo of her at five years old. "He's totally forgotten that I'm a grown woman, perfectly capable of taking care of myself." Then she pointed to her senior photo. "The accident forced some changes. I don't look the same." She shrugged. "I guess I'm not."

Linc couldn't take his eyes off her. He was riveted by the way she touched the things that meant something to her. The deep emotion in her eyes.

He cleared his brain and refocused on the conversation and what he could glean. "Was he so protective before the accident?"

She looked away. But not quickly enough. He got a good look at the misery his question evoked. Linc hated himself for hurting her in any way, but he had to unearth even the most remote memory.

"I…" She met his gaze, the emotion in her eyes under control once more. "I have no memory of my life before." Moving closer to the mantel, she studied the photos of herself as a child and teenager. "Severe head trauma. Global amnesia. It's all gone." As if she couldn't bear to look anymore, she shifted her attention to Linc. "I had to relearn everything. Walking, eating, you name it."

That she had suffered such agony tore him up inside. "Good thing you had family."

"I'm not sure I would've survived without them. I wanted to give up almost every day."

Linc squeezed his fingers into fists in an effort to prevent reaching out to her. "I know that path well myself. But I can't imagine losing every memory."

She folded her arms around her middle. "They say it's gone for good." A small shrug lifted one slender shoulder. "And they're right. I did a ton of research. It's gone. Poof."

"Not even a flicker?" He hated himself for pushing the subject.

She opened her mouth to answer but hesitated. When she'd thought about his question for a few seconds, she said, "Sometimes I feel things if I smell a certain scent. Like Miss Betsy's hand soap."

The confusion must have shown on his face. She

explained, "The lady who runs the Dowe house. Her soap smells like vanilla and coconut. It reminds me of something familiar. I just can't name it."

Vanilla was her favorite candle scent. Soap, too. And she'd loved rubbing coconut oil on her skin whenever they were at the beach. An ache snaked through him. "Any other triggers?"

"Triggers." She nodded, her expression distant. "That's exactly what they call it. Something that evokes a reaction." A downward sweep of her long lashes banished the faraway look in her eyes. "Touch is another trigger. Stronger even than smell, and that's unusual. Sometimes when I'm checking a section of repaired plaster I get this sense of déjà vu. Like I've done it before. Uncle Vince says it's just my imagination."

He would say that. Linc couldn't wait to get his hands on that SOB. "Those feelings could mean there's hope. Medical science isn't perfect. The mind is still largely a mystery. Anything could happen if you're open to the possibility."

She laughed. "You sound like the therapist I used to see."

He made a surprised face. "There's a therapist in Blossom?"

Another laugh combined with a roll of those pretty eyes. "Not here. In Nashville. Dr. Janssen is the best in the field for my situation. My broken brain."

Linc made a mental note of the name. "I'm glad your uncle made sure you had the best treatment." He reached out, couldn't help himself, and smoothed the pad of his thumb over her cheek. Her breath caught, tightening the band of emotions already girding his chest. "And your brain is not broken. It just got banged up a bit."

"I'm sorry." She backed away from him. "I'm supposed to be showing you around, not giving you my sob story." She motioned for him to follow her. "Come on. I'll show you the kitchen and we'll go round up something to eat at my place. I also have tons of color sample chips from the local paint store. You can take them home and figure out what you want."

Linc hung back a few steps to set her at ease after his invasion of her personal space, and just watched her walk. The stride was a little off, not the smooth, sexy gait she'd once had.

But Lori was still there.

No matter that her brain had been emptied of stored memories, she was there. And Linc was going to find her.

Chapter Ten

Wednesday, June 29, 3:00 a.m.

The rattle of metal against wood woke Linc.

His cell vibrated across the bedside table again and he grappled for it in the dark. "Yeah."

"Lopez is on the move."

Keaton. Linc sat up, shoved the hair out of his eyes. "Headed here?"

"Affirmative. A source gave me the heads-up that a private jet filed a flight plan with a small airfield outside Murfreesboro. The flight originates in Bogotá. Arrival time in Tennessee is anticipated as 6:00 a.m. You don't have much time. What's your plan?"

Linc reached for his jeans. "I'm out of here and I'm taking her with me." He set the cell to speaker and placed it on the bedside table so he could pull on his jeans.

"Not that I need to tell you this, but that's kidnapping."

"Who's he gonna call?" Linc wasn't worried about the bastard contacting the authorities, unless it was local cops, and they were in his pocket already.

"She may do the calling," Keaton suggested.

Linc hesitated before pulling his shirt over his head. "She's my wife. Someone else already did the kidnapping. He's the one who needs to be concerned about involving the law."

"The responsibility of substantiating your theory rests on your shoulders, Reece. You can't go off half-cocked and expect to prove your case without evidence. No one knows that better than me."

Linc took a breath to slow his frustration. "I can prove my case. I told you about Mort and about the photos. I'm right. It's her." He'd doubted this whole thing himself at first. But no more. Keaton didn't argue and that was just as well. With those photos, Linc was certain. He dragged on his T-shirt and shoved his feet into his loafers. They were wasting time. He had to get Lori out of here.

"Take I-24 and head south. I'll locate a position for the two of you to lie low. It may take a couple of hours."

"Keep it remote." Lori wouldn't be going voluntarily and Linc had no idea how she would react to being held against her will.

"Reece."

Linc stilled. There was a hint of hesitation or uncertainty in his boss's tone. Something Linc had never heard from the man.

"If Lopez is Marcos," Keaton warned, "he had a reason for going to such extremes to keep Lori for himself. He's not going to give her up without a war."

Fierce determination roared inside Linc. "It's him. But this is one war he won't win." Linc knew Marcos. His reason for taking Lori would be irrelevant at this point. Marcos considered her his and that was all that mattered. Once he'd laid claim, he would never let go.

With Keaton's assurance of finding a safe refuge, Linc ended the call and gathered his gear. He'd arrived in Tennessee prepared to some degree. He had his handgun and ammo and camping gear basics. Sleeping bag, a few bottles of water and energy bars. Not exactly a survival kit but enough to get them started.

All he needed now was her. He checked the time. Three-twenty. There were a number of ways he could draw her out of her home, but those options were saddled with the risk that she might make or receive a call before meeting him. He needed to catch her off guard and keep her that way until some distance stood between them and here.

Breaking and entering was the best option.

He just hoped she'd also forgotten how to put a bullet between a guy's eyes.

3:40 a.m.

MIA'S EYES OPENED. She blinked at the darkness. She'd been dreaming of the accident. The deafening sounds…the heat…the sensation of choking. She had no actual memories of that day. Her therapist had suggested that images and sounds from similar accidents she'd seen in movies or on television had rooted in her subconscious. Whatever the dreams were, she hadn't had them in a long time. But the dream wasn't what woke her. The room felt heavy, as if it were closing in on her, suffocating her. She sat up, threw back the covers and reached for the bedside lamp.

A hand manacled hers, pulled her from the bed even as another clasped firmly over her mouth. She tried to scream but her effort was too late. Her body was crushed into a hard frame by an unyielding forearm. Fear ignited in her veins. She struggled to free herself.

"It's me."

The male voice was a harsh whisper against her hair. Her mind scrambled to identify the voice. When she did, she stopped fighting.

Reece?

"There's a situation. I need your help."

Mia relaxed a little more. What had happened that he felt it necessary to break into her home and snatch her from her bed?

"Don't scream. I'm going to let you go so you can get dressed."

His hands fell away from her. She bolted from him. The move had been instinctive, but she didn't scream. "What's going on?" It took a couple of seconds for her to calm her breathing. Evidently he'd needed that same time to gather his thoughts and give her an answer.

"I can't explain," he said, his voice too quiet, too empty of emotion. "I have to show you."

Renewed fear inched its way up Mia's spine. She'd trusted this stranger too much, too fast. Something was wrong, sure enough—he had lost his mind. Anger kindled, chasing away some of the fear. She reached for the light again and he stopped her just as before.

"No lights."

Mia turned on him. "I don't know what's going on with you, Mr. Reece, but this has gone far enough." The pepper spray her uncle had insisted she keep was in the closet in one of her purses. She'd carried it a few times but the whole idea had seemed ridiculous. Now she wished she had it handy.

"Either get dressed or go as you are," Reece threatened.

"I'll need to get to my closet," she said, feigning cooperation.

He wrapped those long fingers around her arm again. "Lead the way."

Mia looked in the direction of her closet. Her eyes had adjusted to the faint moonlight that filtered in through the curtains. She stepped in that direction, her throat going dry with the possibilities of what Reece intended. Deep down she wasn't actually afraid he would hurt her...though maybe she should be.

With her free hand she opened the closet door. There were no walk-ins in these old homes, unless they'd been added in a remodel. She wished now she'd added one, dead bolt included. Then she could close herself away from him. Mia riffled through the hangers, feeling for a pair of jeans and a blouse. She glanced up at the purses on the top shelf. Since Reece stood right behind her she'd have to figure out how she could dig out the pepper spray.

She wiggled into her jeans. Dang it. She didn't have on a bra beneath the nightgown, but it was pretty dark and her back was to him anyway. Whatever. She yanked off the gown and quickly dragged on the T-shirt.

She took a deep breath. It was time to do something. She faced him, able to just make out his tall frame in the dark. "My shoes are by the bed."

He stepped aside. Not what she'd wanted him to do.

Tension thumped like a pulse in her chest. What now?

"I need my purse." She turned and reached to the top shelf in her closet.

He grabbed her extended arm. "You won't need a purse."

"Fine." She yanked loose from his hold and marched to the bed. Plopping down on the mattress, she reached for the shoes she'd toed off last night.

There had to be something else around here she could use as a weapon. Think! As she tied her shoes, a partial plan started to take shape. She would wait until they were outside, then she'd make a break for it. If she screamed loud enough the neighbor's dog would bark and the whole neighborhood would wake up. Now she wished she'd gotten a dog.

When she stood, Reece took her arm once more and guided her out of the room, down the dark hall and straight to the front door. There he hesitated. "Don't do anything foolish when we get outside. I'm armed."

A stream of true panic poured through her muscles. He had a gun? How had she been so blinded by this guy? She'd sympathized with him and their mutually tortured pasts. He'd seemed so broken, so in need of a friend that she clearly hadn't looked closely enough.

Foolish, Mia. You should have listened to your uncle.

Reece opened her door and they stepped onto the dark porch. The night breeze swept across her face, urging her to run. Instinct warned against allowing him to get her into his SUV.

The two steps down to the sidewalk had her shaking. She needed to do something but she couldn't. Mia felt frozen from the inside out. Why would he do this? Why would he—

"Stop right there, pal."

Beside her, Reece froze.

Mia's brain sluggishly identified the new voice. *Teddy Stewart.* What was he doing here in the middle of the night?

"Let her go."

Reece swayed forward from the waist up as if he'd been jabbed in the back with something. His grasp on Mia's arm relaxed, then fell away.

Mia moved away from him and saw Teddy wielding a shotgun aimed at Reece.

"Put your hands up," Teddy ordered.

"He has a gun." Mia told him. But when her gaze met Reece's, the light from the streetlamp fell over his face and illuminated the ferocity in his blue eyes.

Some foolish part of her regretted what she'd just said. She wanted to take back the words. At the same time his posture and the grim set of his lips sent a distinct fight-or-flight response pumping through her chest. He confused her. Why would he do this?

Teddy snagged Reece's handgun from his waistband. "Get down on your knees."

Reece obeyed, dropping into a surrender stance. His gaze never deviated from Mia's. The ability to breathe eluded her. She'd done the right thing. Why, then, did it feel so wrong?

"Mia."

Her attention swung from Reece to Teddy.

"Get me something to tie him up with."

She snapped out of her coma enough to nod, and seconds later her feet stumbled into motion. "I'll call the chief."

"No."

The snapped word stalled her at the steps. "Why not?" Reece had broken the law. He'd clearly gone over the edge. Calling the police was the right thing to do. Besides, it scared the heck out of her to see Teddy with that shotgun in his hand. In her six years in Blossom she didn't think it had ever left his truck.

"Just get me something," Teddy griped. "Your uncle is on his way here. He wants to talk to this guy first. He says Reece is an old enemy of your father's."

"What?" That couldn't be true. Her father had been a professor at the University of Colorado. He hadn't had any enemies.

"Mia," Teddy blustered, "do what I say."

Mia shook her head. Men. They were all alike. Had to be the boss. She stamped into her house. What was Teddy doing here anyway? Had he been watching Reece or watching her? He was probably doing her uncle's bidding. Uncle Vince had half the town keeping an eye on her. The man was way, way overprotective. But just now she was sort of glad.

What had Reece been thinking?

She had thought he was a nice guy. A little brooding but definitely not mental. She flipped on her bedroom light and snatched a couple of her belts from the closet. Where had Teddy gotten the idea that Reece had somehow known her father? That was ridiculous. Her father had been loved by everyone who knew him. That Reece had known him and wanted to hurt him was totally fictitious. She stormed out of the bedroom…but stopped dead in her tracks.

Reece stood in the living room, glaring at her. Her stomach dropped to her feet. Why hadn't she grabbed the pepper spray? She opened her mouth to scream, but he clapped a hand over it and hauled her toward the door. From the corner of her eye she saw Teddy lying on the sofa. He wasn't moving.

She shook her head and demanded, the words muffled, "What did you do?"

"Your friend will be fine if you stop giving me grief." He tapped the barrel of his gun against his scarred cheek. "Now let's go. No screaming, no running."

Mia threw down the belts, glanced at Teddy to make sure his chest was moving up and down. She walked out the door, down the steps and straight to the SUV parked at the curb. Anger lit in her belly.

He opened the passenger-side door. "Get in."

She glared at him, then did as he ordered.

While he walked around to the driver's side she looked for the keys in the ignition. No such luck. Then she looked for his cell phone. He must have it on him. Great.

He slid into the seat and started the vehicle.

"Where are we going?" He probably wouldn't tell her but that wasn't going to stop her from asking.

"Put your seat belt on."

He pulled away from the curb and accelerated. The way he roared through town was a good thing. Maybe he'd get pulled over and then she would be saved.

Reality set in on the heels of that thought. That

wouldn't happen. The police didn't patrol the streets of Blossom at night.

Because nothing bad ever happened here.

4:48 a.m.

THEY HAD BEEN ON THE ROAD an hour and she hadn't said a word. Linc wanted to explain everything to her but he wasn't sure that was the right thing to do. He hadn't been able to get in touch with the specialist Keaton had suggested. The man was either out of town or he was avoiding Linc's call. He didn't want to risk hurting Lori by taking the wrong steps. The only thing he knew about amnesia was what he'd seen in movies. But this was real life.

His cell vibrated. He dragged it out of his pocket and glanced at the screen to ID the caller. It was Keaton. "Reece."

"Stay south until you see an exit for Winchester. There's a cabin waiting for you in a remote community called Francisco. I'm forwarding the directions to your phone."

That would work. "Any word on his arrival?"

"The plane departed on schedule. I'm leaving for that same airfield now."

That last part stunned Linc. "Come again?"

"You need backup. I'll be in Blossom shortly after Lopez arrives. I'll be watching him."

Linc wasn't about to argue with that. With Keaton on Marcos, he could focus on Lori. "I'll let you know when we arrive at the destination." He slid his phone back into his pocket.

"Why are you doing this?"

The silent treatment appeared to be over. "I'll explain when we get where we're going."

She folded her arms over her chest. "You'll go to jail for this, you know."

"Maybe."

"What went wrong? Did you forget to take your meds yesterday?"

"Funny."

She glared at him. "Actually, it's not. I'm a hostage. That makes you a criminal. You're either crazy or you have some other motive. Like my uncle's money."

Anger simmered in his gut. "I have no interest in your uncle's money."

"Too bad. That means you're crazy."

"Possibly." He'd been told that a time or two.

"Why would Teddy say you're an old enemy of my father's?"

"No idea." That was the one truth he could tell her up front. "I didn't know your father."

She didn't say anything else for a while. The Winchester exit was coming up. He checked the directions on his phone. Less than half an hour to the location Keaton had arranged.

He had plenty of gas and enough bottles of water and snacks to get by. Good thing. He couldn't risk a stop. She might try something and he would not hurt her in any way. His gut warned that she was very much aware of this and that was why she remained fairly calm. The situation was not exactly to his advantage.

"My uncle wouldn't just suddenly come home unless he was very worried." She crossed one leg over the other. Her foot tapped against the console. "He must be certain that you pose a threat of some sort."

Linc posed a threat to her so-called uncle, all right. He'd like nothing better than to see that bastard dead. But Linc had no desire to spend twenty-to-life in prison for ridding the world of a scumbag. He stole a sideways glance at Lori. He had better plans for the next twenty-to-life.

"You have my word," Linc promised, "that you're safe with me." He would die before he'd let her be hurt again in this lifetime.

"Woo-hoo. I feel safer already. I'll just sit back and enjoy the road trip."

That worked for Linc.

Five minutes passed before she broke her silence

again. "No matter what you say, he wouldn't say that for no reason."

"He wants you to be afraid of me." Maybe that was saying too much, but Linc didn't want her getting unreasonably scared or anxious.

"If you didn't know my father, how does my uncle know you?"

She watched him, probably looking for hints of deception. "We met during a joint venture back in L.A." Linc skated on thin ice here. He shouldn't have said so much, but there was no other way to logically answer the question.

"My uncle travels a lot so he may have very well done business on the West Coast," she allowed, her voice stiff with frustration. "But I can't imagine what sort of venture the two of you would have shared. He deals in priceless antiques and artwork. You don't seem like the kind of guy who likes old things."

Linc focused on the driving directions before answering her question. Getting lost wasn't on his agenda. He followed the main street through a sleepy little town called Huntland until the street gave way to a county road that forged a path through farmland. The pastures and fields quickly turned to thick woods as the road narrowed, hugging the mountain on one side and skirting a deep, wooded gulley on the other. Keaton had been right about this place being isolated. All Linc could see for miles were trees and the rocky mountainside.

"Are you ignoring me?"

"I bought the Reid house, didn't I?" That was damned sure old.

"I suspect you had a hidden agenda for that one."

He glanced at her. She was angry. Her chin thrust out and her arms stayed crossed. A smile pulled at his lips. Typical Lori. "You can't prove that."

She arrowed him a furious glare. "I think this is sufficient proof." A hiss of disbelief accompanied a shake of her head.

"You're going to have to trust me."

"I don't think so."

Something in her voice had changed. Tension rippled through Linc, putting him on a higher state of alert. "There are some things I'm not at liberty to disclose at this point," he offered, in hopes of defusing this new agitation he sensed in her. "As soon as I have the go-ahead, you'll know everything."

She turned in the seat to face him. "I'm tired of waiting."

MIA DIDN'T WAIT FOR MORE hedging from Reece. She released her seat belt and dove under the steering wheel. He'd put the gun under the seat. If she could grab it—

He snagged the back of her T-shirt and tried to pull her up. She fought the pull, groped beneath the seat. She had to get the gun. It was the only way to stop him.

The SUV weaved precariously.

Her fingers touched the cold, hard butt of the weapon. He yanked harder. The neck of the T-shirt choked her. She ignored it. She had to get the gun.

Got it! Her fingers tightened on the barrel.

The SUV bumped something and he abruptly released her. Then it tilted and her heart all but stopped. The vehicle was going over the shoulder.

She tried to raise up, but Reece held her down.

The SUV bucked and rocked and Mia screamed. Her hold on the weapon slipped. But right now, grabbing the gun took second place to getting out of this truck alive.

And then, as if the fates mocked her, the SUV plunged forward.

Mia could barely inhale a breath before they hit something and the vehicle came to a jarring stop, pitching her forward. A pop echoed in the truck, and glass shattered. The back of her head banged the underside of the dash as fragments of glass pelted her back.

The world went eerily silent…until Reece swore.

Mia blinked, tried to clear her head. White powder floated down around her like snow.

Strong fingers fisted in her T-shirt and dragged her up. Too late she remembered to reach for the gun.

Reece surveyed her, his gaze frantic. "Are you hurt?"

She stared at him a moment. Maybe she was shaken up or maybe it was the canted position of the SUV, but she couldn't assimilate an answer. The vehicle was pointed nose down. The windshield was shattered. Trees were all around them. Two huge white balloonlike things lay shriveled and impotent on the steering wheel and the dash. Airbags, she realized.

They'd crashed.

"Lori!" He shook her. "Are you hurt?"

She stared at him again. "What?"

He yanked free of his seat belt. His hands were suddenly all over her, roving every inch of her body.

She slapped his hands away. "What the hell are you doing?"

He swiped at his forehead with the back of his hand. Blood smeared across his brow. "Are you hurt?" he demanded again.

Mia performed a quick inventory. She was shaking inside but felt no pain. "I'm okay." She reached toward his head but fell short of touching him. "You're the one who's hurt." This was her fault.

What had she been thinking? They could have been killed.

"It's nothing."

He tried to open the driver's side door, but it didn't budge. He rammed it with his shoulder, once, twice. The door whined as it opened. He climbed out, reached to the floorboard and retrieved his gun.

Mia felt like a fool. She wrenched the handle of her door, but it too failed to budge. She swore, something she rarely did. Ramming her shoulder into the door accomplished nothing but a pain in her arm.

"I can't get out." She looked over the seat at Reece, who was back there doing something.

He moved to the driver's door. "Climb out this way." He offered his hand.

A backpack was slung over his shoulder. Blood wasn't dripping down his forehead but the cut was bloody. She needed her first aid kit. She glanced at his outstretched hand. He'd put new bandages on his fingers. The image of her hand sander lying on the floor amid all that broken glass flashed among the other jumbled thoughts and pictures in her brain.

She took his hand and allowed him to help her out. Emotion churned inside her. She wasn't sure whether she should cry or scream.

Her feet and legs sank into waist-deep underbrush. She looked up at where the road was supposed to be and she gasped. They'd bumped over that shoulder and barreled down a grassy ditch that widened and deepened into a tree-infested ravine.

It was a flat-out miracle they hadn't been killed.

Her knees buckled.

Reece caught her before she went facedown in the bush. He steadied her. "You sure you're okay?"

She stared up into his eyes and realized she felt completely safe with him holding her. It felt safe and…familiar.

The gun in his waistband grazed her stomach, shattering the confusing sensations. She jerked out of his hold, swayed but quickly steadied herself. "I told you I'm fine." She turned her attention back to where the road should be, but it wasn't actually visible from here. The only thing on her mind right now was getting up there and getting help.

Mia plowed through the brush and started the long climb to the top of the ravine. She grabbed handfuls of the wild plant life to pull her way upward.

Reece stayed right behind her.

Mia didn't give one flip. As soon as she reached the road she was going to run as fast as she could back toward that little town they'd passed through.

She didn't care if he chased her or shot her.

She was running.

Chapter Eleven

Reece reached the road first.

He waited for Mia.

Out of breath, she dragged herself up to the rocky shoulder. Any notion that she was in shape went out the proverbial window. Catching her breath would be essential before making a run for it. She swiped her hands on her jeans and looked around. They were in the middle of nowhere! The mountain bellied up to the pavement on one side of the road; the gulley gutted the other side. Trees camouflaged everything else, including the sky, but it was daylight. Barely.

"This way."

Mia spun on her heel and stared in disbelief at the man who'd dragged her all this way. "I don't know what you're thinking! We are in the middle of nowhere! The car is destroyed and town is miles back that way." She hitched her thumb in the direction opposite the one he'd chosen. "Whatever scheme you were planning you need to rethink the situation. It's over." She took a breath and started toward town.

Stupidly she had hovered on some mental fence about whether to feel sorry for him or come to terms with the idea that he was off his rocker. She'd sat like a zombie in the passenger seat while he'd driven for two hours. How could she have been so thick-skulled? So delusional? He was not some poor guy in need of her sympathy and support. No matter that he'd suffered as she had, lost so much, he wasn't to be trusted.

Even as her brain latched onto that conclusion, her heart balked. What was wrong with her? Stock-holm syndrome, apparently. Not that she would have jumped out of a moving vehicle, but at least she could've tried harder to talk some sense into him.

Idiot.

Strong arms wrapped around her. "I said this way."

Before she could wrench loose, Reece had flung her over his shoulder and started marching in the other direction, away from town.

Mia screamed. Then she pounded his back, for all the good it did with the danged backpack in the way. He held her legs firmly against his chest.

"Scream all you want." He tightened his hold. "No one's going to hear."

He was right. She snapped her mouth shut. Trees

were all she could see. The neglected road was deserted and silence was the only sound for miles.

She growled ferociously and thumped his back with both fists. Every swear word she'd ever heard and some she hadn't even realized she knew gushed off her tongue as if she'd spent the last year living on a ship filled with salty sailors. When she'd exhausted her crude vocabulary, she sucked in a desperate, frustrated breath.

"That was interesting."

Her eyes bulged with another blast of anger and she cut loose with a second tirade.

"Guess that quiet, naive artisan persona wasn't the real you."

Exhausted with struggling and yelling, she couldn't summon an adequate comeback. Instead, she slumped against him, one cheek pressed against the canvas backpack, her face crammed into his shirt and the taut body it clung to. She hated how her own body reacted to his male scent. And it had to be all him, no cologne could possibly smell that naturally sexy. Dammit. Dammit. Dammit.

Fury boiled in her belly. She was a hostage and she couldn't even muster the proper reaction. In spite of all this, she wasn't afraid of him hurting her. If that had been his intent he certainly could have done so already.

It was official. He wasn't crazy. She was.

Maybe it had been so long since she had experienced any excitement in her life that she was desperate for it. Or, more likely, the brain damage she'd suffered had stolen her ability to distinguish good from bad, intelligent from imprudent.

The sound of gravel crunching beneath his shoes snagged her attention. Mia raised her head to stare at the road, and a frown tugged her lips downward. He'd turned off the paved road onto dirt and gravel. Before she could demand an explanation, he bent forward and settled her onto her feet.

He restrained her arm with his hand to ensure she didn't try running. She wasn't going to waste her time. Paying attention to the details of their route was far more important. When she managed an escape she would need to remember the route. Mia had never been to this part of Tennessee. This far south they were probably very close to the Alabama state line. Truth was, she didn't travel much at all. Occasionally she went to South America with her uncle but always on his plane, and never for a minute was she out of his sight.

She stumbled but Reece caught her. Their gazes bumped and she realized something while she looked into those concerned blue eyes. She wasn't really living. No relationship knocks, no falling, emotionally or otherwise, no nothing. She was just poor, sweet little Mia. Fragile Mia. The one who needed looking after.

Her lips tightened with resentment and anger. She yanked her arm free of Reece's hold. "What do you want from me?"

Surprise, then confusion crossed his face.

"Just spell it out. Do you want something from me or from my uncle?"

For a moment Reece simply stared at her. Then he said, "I want him to pay for what he's done."

Mia lifted her chin defiantly. "So this is about money." Disappointment dropped like a rock into her stomach. She was a fool for believing on any level that this man was basically good.

Reece shook his head. "His money has nothing to do with my motives. I want him to finally answer for his crimes."

Crimes? "What're you talking about?" She planted her fists on her hips. "I doubt my uncle has so much as an outstanding parking ticket." His accusation was completely off the wall.

Reece started walking again, just turned his back and kept going.

Mia stormed after him, the gravel crunching under her shoes. "He hasn't committed any crimes," she said, but Reece didn't slow down. "Are you listening to me?"

"Your uncle is a dangerous man." Reece said this

without so much as a glance at her and with hardly any emotion in his tone. That part wasn't exactly out of character.

"I don't believe you." She walked faster to match his stride. The whole town of Blossom loved Vincent Lopez. A whole town couldn't be wrong. Mia wasn't wrong. This man—this stranger out of nowhere— was wrong.

"I can't fix that."

Fix that? Was he insinuating something about her loss of memory? Or her intelligence level? "I don't need you to fix anything."

Reece stopped and turned to face her, effectively blocking her path. "That didn't come out right."

She wanted to tell him where to go but she just stared into those dark blue eyes. They drew her, made her want to keep looking until she was lost inside him…was a part of him. Yes, she was definitely crazy.

"The man you know as Vincent Lopez is a wanted fugitive and I will bring him to justice."

Mia moved back a step. Reece couldn't be serious. "That's impossible." The entire concept was ludicrous. Who was this man? He'd shown up in her life, made her like him and now he told her this. "You don't know what you're talking about."

"Like I said," he grumbled as he started up the

gravel road once more, "I can't fix this. I don't even know how to begin to make you see."

She considered turning around and running the other way but she couldn't. Reece had to understand. Her uncle had saved her, had been there for her when no one else was. She owed him everything.

"Vincent Lopez supports dozens of charities." She lengthened her stride to keep up with Reece. "Before he returned to Blossom, the town was dying. He brought it back to life. The people here see him as a hero. I see him as a hero."

"Have you ever wondered why he spends so much time in South America?"

Mia wished the canopy of trees would open up and let the morning sun through. She hugged her arms around herself. A chill had invaded her bones in spite of the uphill trek. "He has family there and he specializes in—"

"Yeah, yeah, I know." Reece marched onward, his determined strides matching his tone. "Antiques and art. Doesn't that seem a little clichéd to you?"

His responses confused her. Vince shipped all sorts of beautiful pieces from South America. Some he sold in Blossom's shops, others went to buyers all over the country. Mia had marveled over many of them. "Nothing you said makes sense to me." Another concept materialized in her whirling thoughts.

"Are you a cop?" Had he mentioned his occupation? At the moment she couldn't remember.

"Not anymore."

She hurried to get in front of him, almost lost her footing in the loose gravel. "You used to be a cop?" He'd said that he and her uncle had worked a joint venture in L.A. That couldn't be. The man she knew, who had dragged her back to the land of the living, wouldn't be involved in criminal activity.

"In L.A."

Something like apprehension logjammed her throat. She stood very still, waiting for it to pass. A few yards ahead she could see part of a roof. Reece kept going in that direction.

She didn't want to go.

Mia's feet seemed to mire in the dirt and gravel, sinking into an imaginary muck. Every instinct warned that if she kept going, that if she listened to anything more Reece had to say, her life would be turned upside down. She had worked so hard to rebuild her life. Starting over again felt insurmountable…overwhelming.

Reece had to be wrong.

A sharp, stabbing pain pierced her skull. Mia grabbed her head, squeezed her eyes shut. This was all wrong. She took deep, slow breaths. The headaches had been gone for years now, until the last few days.

Until he'd shown up.

The pain passed and she opened her eyes. Reece looked so far away. She put one foot in front of the other and forced her legs to cooperate.

She didn't want to know any of this but somehow she couldn't stop moving toward that end.

Reece drew her like the flame drew a moth.

She needed him…she just didn't know why or how.

THE CABIN WAS RUSTIC but it would do. It had only one large room and no running water, as far as Linc could see. He pulled the coverings off two windows to let in some light. Dust particles floated in the air. An old tattered sofa, two equally ragged chairs and a wood table surrounded by rickety-looking straight-back chairs cluttered the space. He peeled off the backpack and let it drop to the floor. He'd forgotten the sleeping bag. Looked like they would need it. Walking back for it wouldn't be a big deal except for having to drag Lori along.

He shook his head. He'd called her that. A mistake he couldn't make again.

"What evidence do you have?"

She stood in the open doorway looking weary and fragile. He ached to hold her and to reassure her but that would only lead to him saying more. He'd already said too much. Far too much.

He reached into the backpack and pulled out a bottle of water and offered it to her. "Rest for a bit. We'll talk about that later."

She stamped across the creaky wood floor and stood toe-to-toe with him. "You said my uncle is a criminal. What evidence do you have?" She flung out her arms. "You're a former cop. You surely understand the need for legitimate evidence."

She was mad as hell. Her lips were tight with fury, her shoulders literally shook.

"He operated one of the largest drug cartels in the western part of the United States. The explosion I told you about was on his yacht." *Don't go too far.* "A competitor wanted him out of the business. The man you call your uncle was supposed to die that day."

She drew in a startled breath. As if the ramifications of the information shook her a second time, her eyes rounded with realization. "The same explosion that killed your wife. That injured you."

Reece had to turn away. He grabbed the backpack and crossed to the table. One by one, he placed the contents of the pack on the table, mentally inventorying each. Anything to distract his mind and his hands.

"I'm right, aren't I?" She joined him at the table, her relentless gaze cutting through him.

He set the last bottle of water on the table. "Yes."

He met her insistent gaze, hated the pain that glimmered there at his answer.

"You want vengeance." The words were scarcely a whisper. "That's why you came. It wasn't about the house you bought, it was about vengeance."

He wanted to say no, that it was about her. But, in truth, vengeance played a part, too. He hadn't known until he'd arrived in Blossom and learned the facts of how she came to be there. If it would stop her persistent questions for now, he would say whatever she wanted to hear. He could only take so much.

"Maybe. Mostly I'd like to see justice served." He exhaled. His insides wouldn't stop quaking. His gut was tied in knots. Years of feeling nothing at all were suddenly blitzing him with all those suppressed emotions.

She blinked, took another of those ragged breaths. "What kind of evidence do you have?"

"The photos in his house." She was pushing and he couldn't go there. "I recognized him." Why didn't she let it go?

She bit her bottom lip until it was red. His body lurched with the need to lean down and soothe that mistreated flesh with his mouth…with his tongue. He yearned to touch her.

"Then you weren't sure he was there when you came to Blossom. Not until you saw the photos."

She just kept pushing. "I had reason to believe he was there."

"What reason?" She glared up at him, uncertainty shadowing her face.

Five, then ten trauma-filled seconds elapsed. "I have to make a call."

He didn't give her time to react. Linc walked out. He couldn't breathe until he was a dozen yards from the cabin. He dragged his cell from his pocket and checked the screen. "Damn." No service. He should have expected that. Came with the territory when lying low in remote locations.

The way the SUV was hidden in that gulley, it wasn't likely that any passersby would spot it and report it. That was good and bad. Good that the cops wouldn't be snooping around but bad that he and Mia had no transportation. He had a feeling there wouldn't be much traffic out here, in any event. Wasn't the worst-case scenario. They weren't that many miles from town.

"It's me, isn't it? That's why he tried to protect me from you."

Linc hesitated before turning around. She stood on the porch. A memory of Lori, standing on the porch of that old house they'd eventually bought and yelling at him because he wasn't as excited about it as she was, rolled through his mind. She had thrown her hands up and paced back and forth until he'd walked straight up to her and kissed her. Then he'd promised her they would do anything she wanted.

Making her happy was all that had mattered to him.

He slid the phone back into his pocket and racked his brain for an answer that would satisfy her and not take this too far. There was only one way to do that. "You were part of it." He walked toward her, adopted a don't-care attitude. "I knew getting close to you could work." He stopped at the porch, didn't take the one step up since she stood directly in his path, and stared into her eyes. "Luring prey always requires bait."

She slapped him hard. Just as quickly she held her hand with the other as if the slap hurt her as much or more than it did him.

MIA'S HEAD WAS SPINNING as she held her hand close to her chest. The stinging wasn't the problem. It was that other indescribable sensation she felt every time she touched him. The insatiable need to be close to him. To touch more of him and learn the secret of that power he seemed to hold over her.

"You used me." Her lips trembled. She hated herself for feeling weak. Hated him for what he made her feel. She was the reason her uncle was in trouble. After all he'd done for her.

"I did what I had to do." With that, he stepped past her and went inside.

Mia stood there, reeling with indecision. How could she believe that her uncle was a drug lord without proof? No jury would convict a man without evidence. Certainly she would not. Why wouldn't Reece tell her what proof he had, other than the fact her uncle looked like the man he sought? It wasn't right.

Mia closed her eyes, steadied her mind. She needed answers. She had to be stronger than this. Inside the cabin, she found Linc downing a bottle of water. "You said you used to be a cop. Why is an ex-cop luring prey?" Renewed anger at how he'd used her blistered her senses.

Reece placed the empty bottle on the table. "Because he took something from me."

Another shock radiated through her. Her gaze dropped to his injured leg, then traveled up the length of his muscled thighs and chest to his face. The scar. There was no need to ask. He'd named the number of surgeries required after the explosion he had survived. She'd seen the limp. His scars, physical and mental, were mementos from that awful tragedy.

And his wife. She had died in that explosion.

"You said a competitor was responsible for the explosion." Even if her uncle was the man he spoke of, and he absolutely could not be, someone else had caused the explosion. The shaking started again, in her knees. It climbed up her thighs, spread over her chest, down her arms and to her fingers.

"You think that makes it any less his fault?"

Linc's posture was so rigid he looked ready to snap. Mia swallowed, moistened her lips. She shook her head. "You still don't have tangible evidence that my uncle is the man you seek." Reece was confused. He'd made a mistake. His grief had driven him to do these things. Mia was right. Lincoln Reece was a good man. He just needed help to see that the past couldn't be changed. What was done was done. If he had evidence that Vincent Lopez was the monster that he spoke of, he should use it to make his case through legal channels.

Mia tried to garner strength from her own words but her heart pounded so hard the blood roared in her ears. She waited for his next move. She wanted to fix him…to fix this. It was unreasonable, completely illogical, but she couldn't help it. He seemed so alone. So broken. "Looks can be deceiving," she added when he said nothing. "It's what's beneath that makes the man." She needed him to see that. To take her back home and straighten all this out. Her uncle would explain everything. Confusion elbowed its way back into her conclusions. Her uncle had told Teddy that Reece was dangerous. An old enemy of her father's. Why would he lie? There was no reason for a man who had nothing to hide to be deceitful.

"I found the evidence I need."

Mia's attention flew back to Reece, but he refused to look at her. Her throat tightened, went painfully dry. "The photo isn't—"

Reece turned toward her, the feral expression on his face making her truly afraid for the first time since she'd awakened to discover someone in her room.

"I found what he took from me." His attention dropped to the floor. "No one else was there or had the means to take the one thing that mattered to me."

His wife. The blood drained to Mia's feet, leaving her as cold as death. "You said your wife is dead." The thumping in her chest threatened to split open her sternum.

Her body was never found.

Reece said nothing. He walked out, left Mia alone with the unthinkable throbbing in her skull.

Seven years ago.

Explosion.

The car accident had been seven years ago.

She remembered nothing from that day or from her entire existence before.

Hundreds of memories she had made since flashed one after the other in her mind, making her sway. Her uncle bringing her to Blossom after rehab was over. Her aunt Gloria's smile. Her hard work for months to help Mia fit in the real world again. Her first birthday celebration after the accident…first Christmas. Day after day of trying to remember. Night after night of dreaming things she couldn't fully recall or make sense of the next morning. The moments of déjà vu after a certain scent or touch.

Lori! Are you hurt?

Reece had called her Lori back in the SUV. After the crash.

Numbness replaced the cold that had filled her. She was out the door before she realized she had moved, standing behind Reece on the porch.

She opened her mouth to speak but nothing came out. Fear had a choke hold on her voice. After inhaling a deep breath, she tried again. "What was your wife's name?"

He didn't turn around. He continued staring at the trees, or something Mia couldn't see.

"Tell me." She dragged in a bolstering breath. "I need to know."

Reece turned around slowly. Mia's world seemed to turn upside down in unison with his movements. She told herself to brace but she didn't possess the physical or mental ability.

"Lori." His gaze locked with hers. "My wife's name is Lori."

Lori! Are you hurt?

Because he took something from me… I found what he took from me.

Air would not enter her lungs. The wood porch boards shifted and swayed beneath her though she hadn't moved. Her vision narrowed until it encompassed nothing but his face…then his eyes.

"You think I'm Lori," she whispered. The trees moved in a circle around her. "You believe I'm your wife."

He said something but Mia couldn't make out the words. The spinning had sucked her into a vortex that grew deeper and deeper until everything else vanished.

Chapter Twelve

Slade Keaton waited for Jim Colby to debark the Colby Agency jet. Jim's excuse for hanging back had been that he needed to instruct the pilot to remain standing by until additional orders were relayed. Slade suspected that Colby actually wanted to give Lucas Camp an update.

Even before Slade had passed along Lopez's flight plan to Reece, he had called the Colby Agency for support. After all, that was what friends did, wasn't it? Provided support in times of need? There were others Slade could have called, but phoning the Colby Agency had killed two birds with one stone, so to speak. Slade acquired the air transport he needed and he solidified his relationship with the Colbys on yet another level.

Jim Colby descended the steps from the plane. Blond, blue-eyed, he looked more like his father, James, than his esteemed mother, Victoria. Like Slade, he bore the unmistakable marks of a harrowing past. Kidnapped by an enemy of the Colbys at age seven, Jim had been physically abused and mentally tormented for nearly two decades. His return some six years ago had been accompanied by much drama and emotion. Now, however, that was all behind him. Jim was a golden one once more. Cherished by his mother, respected by his colleagues and doted on by his stepfather, Lucas Camp.

Slade relaxed his clenched fists. Jim and all those around him would know soon enough what kind of man Lucas Camp really was.

Jim approached Slade, his expression grim. "Our contact at the Bureau is going to attempt to locate a photo of Lopez for comparison with the file on Marcos. Increased drug activities originating in the central Tennessee area have been on DEA's watch list for the past three years. This may be the break they need for pinpointing the source." He gestured to a dark sedan parked near the hangar. "That's our ground transportation."

The drive to Blossom was less than an hour. They were mere minutes behind Lopez.

"I appreciate your help, Jim." Slade followed him to the car. "This situation is quite precarious.

I'm hoping to track down the right specialists for Reece's wife's condition. He'll need all the backup I can provide, even when we bring his old enemy to justice."

Jim hesitated at the driver's door. "If her condition involves brainwashing, I know the right people for that. If it's amnesia, the Colby Agency can assist with finding the right doctors. I'll ask Victoria to conduct some preliminary inquiries."

Slade nodded. "I know Reece will appreciate any help in the matter. He's waited a long time for the truth." As had Slade. But that was another matter for another time.

After settling behind the wheel, Jim asked, "Lopez has no security team on the ground in Blossom?"

Slade reached for his seat belt. "Reece was not aware of one. My contact indicated that two other passengers were traveling with Lopez. Bodyguards, if I had my guess. Reece mentioned a local who appeared to do Lopez's bidding. Ted Stewart. Reece indicated Stewart was not a real threat, just a regular Joe looking for extra cash or brownie points with the man who owns the town." Slade considered something else Reece had relayed. "That said, Stewart was armed when he attempted to intercept Reece."

"Noted," Jim acknowledged.

Slade would have preferred touching base with Reece when he and Jim had touched down at the airfield, but the call hadn't gone through. It wasn't unusual for cell service to be lacking in remote, mountainous areas. Reece could take care of himself as long as Slade and Jim handled things on this end.

The conversation lulled for long enough to become awkward. Slade was no fool. He recognized that the Colbys were suspicious of him. As they well should be. The position of power and prestige they had attained made the Colbys prime targets. Caution was necessary.

"How's your caseload going at the shop?" Jim asked.

Ah, small talk. "The Equalizers are staying busy. I'm contemplating employing two additional investigators. I've already replaced two of my men. I suspect I'll be losing Reece, as well. He'll want to focus solely on his personal life." Jonathan Foley had made a similar decision. Dakota Garrett's departure had been for very different reasons. He was not happy that Slade had opted not to be entirely open with the Colby Agency after Victoria's recent abduction. Slade was braced for that to come back to haunt him.

"It's difficult to find investigators for the kind of work the Equalizers do," Jim agreed. "That level of commitment to deep cover is problematic once personal ties come into play. You generally lose staff."

Slade had never understood that emasculating need to get tied down with marriage and kids. Life was complex enough without the unnecessary baggage.

"There are still men out there," Slade said, "who value the mission above all else."

Jim braked at an intersection and turned to Slade. "Speaking from personal experience, you have to wonder about a man who loves nothing else," Jim said frankly. "Don't you agree?"

The unspoken challenge hung in the air. Slade smiled. "Perhaps." He faced forward as Jim resumed the journey.

Some truths were best left unrevealed until the time was right.

Chapter Thirteen

Linc carefully lowered Lori onto the sofa. Her respiration was steady. Surely she'd come around any second now. God, he hoped so. With no cell service and no transportation, his options for getting help were limited. What else could he do?

He grabbed a bottle of water from the table and peeled off his shirt. With a little water soaked into one corner of the material, he used the shirt like a cloth to pat her face. Her skin didn't feel overly warm. The truth he'd revealed had simply overwhelmed her. He should have been more careful. He'd tried to hold back but she'd just kept pushing, demanding answers. Not that he could blame her. He'd invaded her life, then kidnapped her without any sort of explanation.

He traced the outline of her soft cheek. His fingers clenched to restrain the urge to touch her lips. He had been so sure he'd lost her forever. But she was right here. He wanted to hold her close against his chest and never let her go, just to be sure no one ever took her from him again.

But she wasn't his anymore.

Marcos had stolen her from him. Linc couldn't get right with that reality. Sure, the old bastard had loved to gawk at Lori. He'd considered her his, but no more so than he had Linc or any of his other subordinates in the cartel. At least, not to Linc's knowledge. Lori would have told him if Marcos had approached her in any way.

Her past—her entire identity—was lost. Her only history was as Mia Grant. She had formed bonds and made a life that didn't include Linc and her twenty-three years prior to the explosion. If those memories never returned, was there any compelling reason for her to want to be Lori Reece? Or to have Linc in her life? The misery that welled inside him pressed against his heart—the organ he had long thought dead to emotion.

Beneath his touch, Lori stirred, her eyes opened. She blinked, then zeroed in on him. Fear or apprehension flared in those golden-brown depths. "I need to go home." She scrambled up, forcing him aside.

Linc stayed back, let her regain her bearings.

She walked out onto the porch, surveyed the woods that crowded around them, then stared back at him. He shook out his shirt and pulled it back on.

The damp spot was irrelevant. He wanted her comfortable. Having a half-naked man standing around wouldn't help. That he was her husband didn't count at the moment.

Lori came back inside, grabbed the bottle of water on the sofa and drank down half the contents. She screwed the top back on and tossed it aside. Drawing in a deep breath, she met his gaze. "Granted, my name and history were laid out for me by my aunt and uncle and—" she visibly braced "—I have no way of proving the validity of what they told me, but I also have no reason to doubt it." Her confidence seemed to build as she spoke.

Linc wasn't sure what she wanted him to say, if anything.

"You believe differently." Her voice shook. "I'd like to know why." Before he could speak, she added, "And don't use those pictures you saw at my...uncle's house as your reasons. Just because I look like someone else doesn't mean I am that person."

Fair enough. He gestured to the sofa. "Do you want to sit?"

She shook her head, threaded her fingers through her hair.

Then he started his story. "My wife's body was never found. Neither were several others. More than a dozen people died that day, the remains of only five were recovered. Part of me held on to the idea that my wife wasn't dead."

That shaking he'd heard in her voice carried through to the rest of her. He saw it in her hands, in her slender shoulders. He hated doing this to her.

"Go on." She infused a good deal of courage into those two words.

"I looked for you—for my wife—long after the recovery teams had stopped. Finally I gave up." He shrugged, the movement as listless as he felt at the moment. "I packed all the photos, everything related to our life together, and stored it. The only other person who had access to the stuff was my former partner, Mort Fraley." Linc watched for any sign of recognition in her eyes or posture. Nothing. "Then I moved on." He sat down in the nearest chair, not trusting the steadiness of his legs. "Or tried to. Mostly I drifted from place to place, job to job."

"Why did you come to Blossom now?" Her lips quivered.

He had to look away. "Last week Mort, my old friend and former partner, came to see me in Chicago." Linc glanced at her. "That's where I live now. He told me he'd seen you. That you were alive." Linc shook his head. Even now it sounded crazy. "He pushed me to come see for myself. So I did."

"Just because I look like her," she countered again, "doesn't mean anything."

"Your nose is different." He dared to study her face. "The brow. The slightest changes."

She touched her face as he spoke.

"But your eyes. Lips." He had to look away again. "Your voice. The way you move. All the same."

She was the one looking away then.

"Still," he continued, since she didn't advise him otherwise, "I wasn't convinced. I needed to know more before I took any action."

"That's why you bought the house and sought out my help with renovations you didn't really care about." The resentment in her tone fell short of appearing on her face. She looked scared and alone.

"Yes."

"Is there anything else about me that reminds you of her?"

"Your work."

She stilled, clearly surprised. "The plasterwork?"

He nodded. "Lori loves old houses. We finally bought one and she learned to do a lot of the cosmetic repairs herself." A smile pulled at his lips. "She was a natural at it. *California Living* did a feature on her restorative work, using her maiden name, of course." She had been so happy that day. Linc would do anything to make her that happy again.

Her movements stilted, she walked to the sofa and

sat down. "How can my work prove anything? It's coincidence."

"The way you touch the plaster and move your trowel is exactly the same. I watched her just like I watched you. There's a rhythm to what you do. It's almost like a dance."

"Wait. You were a cop," she countered, her tone argumentative. "Why was she on the boat that day?"

"We were both detectives. We were under deep cover as a couple in Marcos's family."

"Marcos." She frowned. "That's who you think my uncle is."

"Juan Marcos." He let her know with his eyes that he wasn't relenting on that one. "I know he is Juan Marcos. The feds have a file a mile thick on him. Proving who he is will be easy." Linc wanted him to pay. The sooner the better.

She moistened her lips. "You can't be certain of what you say about me. I couldn't have been a cop. I don't even know how to hold a weapon. I couldn't shoot one if my life depended on it."

He was certain. He just couldn't prove it. "You walked before," he countered, "but after the accident you had to relearn. There's no reason for you to know about guns now since you didn't relearn that skill."

"That doesn't prove anything except that you were listening to what I told you about my recovery."

"The photos of you as a child," he explained, "are photos of my wife. They were stolen from my storage unit back in L.A."

She shot up from the sofa. "That's impossible." She started to pace the room. "Those are me. I grew up in Boulder. Went to school there until the accident. Those photos were with me every day of rehabilitation."

As much as he wanted to move, Linc kept his seat. He didn't want to appear threatening. "Where are the photos of you with your family?"

She whirled to glare at him. "My uncle has them. He keeps them put away so I don't focus on the past."

"You've seen them?"

"Of course."

"Were there any of you and your parents all together?"

The rhythm of her pacing changed, as if she'd lost focus.

"I have photos of you with your real parents, Nadine and Ellis Counts."

Her pattern of pacing altered once more. "Where are these people? What do they have to say about this?"

"They died in a car accident when you were in college." He paused to let that news sink in. "You have no other living relatives, at least none that you ever mentioned. Both your parents were only children, just like you. Sound familiar?"

"Lots of people are only children. Lots die in car accidents." Her hands landed on her hips. "You can't seriously believe that a handful of common qualities proves your theory."

He stood, couldn't sit still any longer. "I have hundreds of photos of you—the you in the photos we saw on that mantel last night—with Nadine and Ellis Counts, from the day you were brought home from Los Angeles General to the day you moved into your first apartment while a sophomore at UCLA. Your wedding day with me. Our first place together. I could go on and on."

She backed up a step as if she could escape his words. "Why didn't you bring them?"

"They're in L.A." The hollowness in her eyes and voice cut him like a knife. "There was no reason to bring any. I wasn't sure about you until I came and saw you on that ladder repairing plaster."

"Where did you meet your wife?" She was trembling again.

"On the job. I had just made detective."

She looked away. "Where did you get married?"

He smiled. "You insisted we get married on the beach in Malibu. You love the sun and the sand, the sound of the water lapping the shore. You—"

"How long were you married?" she interrupted.

"Next month will be eight years." He was not going to discount the last seven years. She was his wife. She was alive and, until she chose otherwise, they were still married. That possibility twisted the knife already thrust deep in his chest.

"What about fingerprints or DNA?" She stiffened her shoulders. "You must have something more conclusive than the photos and your personal conclusions."

"You have no family so there's no comparison for a DNA test. Your prints were lost in a gas leak explosion at the hall of records just one year after the accident."

"That's convenient."

"Yes, it is. Very convenient for the man who brought you to Tennessee and gave you a whole new identity." Damn that bastard.

She crossed her arms over her chest. "Nothing you've said sounds familiar to me." She lifted her chin defiantly. "You aren't familiar to me. I've never even been to the West Coast."

"I'm not trying to force you to accept anything." He took a moment, reached for calm. "This is something you have to come to terms with on your own or with professional help. All I'm asking is that you be open to whatever can be done to determine the truth." He had no idea what that would be, other than working with the right specialists and looking at the photos of her life. Assuming Mort hadn't done away with all of them. A mixture of frustration and fury churned inside Linc. How could the man have done this?

"I need to think."

She walked past him and out the door. He let her go and didn't follow. This was a lot to absorb. He wasn't sure if giving her this information was the right thing to do, but he'd had no other choice.

Now all he could do was wait.

The next move was hers.

MIA WALKED TO THE TREE LINE. Her head throbbed, her chest felt ready to explode. How could any of this be true? Vince had treated her like a daughter. And Gloria... Dear God, she would be beside herself with Mia missing. She could prove what Mia said. She had been there every step of the way during Mia's recovery.

She forced herself to think. How could the last seven years have been some movie-of-the-week plot? Vince had never been anything but kind and loving toward her. Why would he have done something so heinous? If not her parents, who were the people in the photographs? If, as Reece said, his old partner had provided actual photos of this Lori person, why not provide pictures of her with her parents?

Lori's parents had been killed in a car crash just like Mia's. Could be coincidence. The love of historic homes and the unexpected ability to repair plaster... so what? Three coincidences did not a conspiracy make.

Mia sat down on the ground. She didn't care that sticks and gravel and leaves jabbed at her bottom. She needed to feel something real. She closed her eyes and inhaled the sweet country air. The hint of a breeze whispered across her face. Life would be so easy if she could just remember. But that wasn't going to happen. The experts, and she had seen plenty, had all agreed that the damage to her brain had been far too significant for any stored memories to return.

For seven years that had been the case. Not a single true memory. Oh, she had the occasional moment of déjà vu. Who didn't? Those moments she experienced when exposed to certain scents and touches were so rare that she felt certain they didn't actually count.

Inside, a quiet consumed her, then like flashes of a camera, memories invaded her mind. Shaking Reece's hand that first time...touching his fingers when she'd applied the bandages...his scent when she was really close to him...feeling overwhelmed... No one had ever evoked those emotions of familiarity and safety the way he did. In fact, no one had caused a single one of those reactions. The scents and touches that had, in the past, were not related to a person. They had always occurred when she'd touched a certain fabric or item, or smelled some cooking spice or a scented candle.

She wrung her hands. Even she had to admit that aspect of this insanity was significant.

Mia glanced at the cabin. Reece hadn't followed her outside, which she appreciated. She needed space and time to digest all that he'd told her. To come up with rationales that negated his accusations.

For years she had fought for a normal life, learning to walk, read, write, how to fit in to the world again. She couldn't let that be stripped away. This life, these memories were all she had.

Mia climbed to her feet and dusted off her jeans. This was the only life she had. She wasn't giving it up without undeniable proof. Starting over was hard. She couldn't climb that mountain again unless she was sure the journey was the only right one.

Reece had waited inside but he'd been watching her from the window. The expectant expression on his face made her sad. She had never met a man as sad and lost as Lincoln Reece. Part of her—not the Mia Grant part but the wholly woman part— wanted to reach out to him. To help him find his way. How could she, when she wasn't even certain of her own?

She had to know for sure. "What about dental records?" She'd had some restorative work done after the accident, but mostly just cosmetic stuff. "Surely those weren't lost, too."

"I have those."

He brought dental records but no photos? Her face must have telegraphed her surprise.

"I had them digitally downloaded to my phone after I saw you for the first time."

"Then we need a dentist." She smoothed her hair and straightened her T-shirt. "Let's go."

A frown trenched across his brow. "Come again?"

"We'll walk back to that little town. They probably have a dentist." The more she thought about it, the more determined she got. She wanted this part over. Whatever her uncle had or had not done, she would deal with later. Reece stared at her as if she'd announced some unthinkable news. "It's not that far," she said. "If we're lucky someone will come along and give us a ride."

"Keeping you safe is my main objective right now."

His hesitation frustrated her. "I'm not afraid of my uncle. What I am afraid of is you." The last was truer than she wanted him to know. Strangely, it had nothing to do with fear for her safety.

He reached for the handgun on the table and tucked it into his waistband at the small of his back, then pulled his shirt down to cover it. The stretch of the fabric drew her gaze to his broad chest and she shivered. *Stop, Mia.* She had to remain objective. This was too important to get distracted.

"Let's go."

She didn't wait for him. She just walked out the door. As determined as she was to know the truth, she was even more terrified.

10:50 a.m.

THE ROUTE FROM HUNTLAND to the cabin had taken ten minutes to drive. Walking took close to two hours. Not a single vehicle had passed. Linc worried about Lori walking the seven or eight miles but it was he favoring his bum leg by the time they reached their destination. Not to mention, every step had been made in silence. He had considered a dozen ways to start up a conversation but he'd dismissed the idea each time.

She didn't want to talk. Not to him, anyway.

The small town not only had a dentist's office, but there was a café, a school, a medical clinic, a post office, supermarket and at least two convenience stores. They had walked by each and every one.

Linc opened the door to the modest dental office and waited for Lori to enter. Before going in, she met his gaze for the first time since they'd left the cabin. That brief look confirmed just how terrified she was. He felt helpless and sick to his stomach that there wasn't an easier way to do this.

The receptionist smiled. "May I help you?"

Lori looked to him to handle the question. "We don't have an appointment," he confessed, "but we need to see the dentist."

The receptionist frowned. "Have you been seen here before?"

"No." He glanced at Lori. "We're from out of town. And we have a problem." His explanation sounded lame even to him. For the last couple of hours his mind had been on Lori's well-being and how he'd failed to do this right, rather than on how to accomplish the next step.

"I'm sorry but we don't have any openings this morning." The receptionist scanned her appointment book. "We might be able to work you in late this afternoon." She looked from Linc to Lori and back. "What's the nature of the problem?"

That would be the sticky part.

Lori moaned. "I have a missing cap and it's killing me." She held her jaw. "We're on vacation and I don't think I can stand this another minute, much less another day." She groaned even louder.

Astonished, Linc stared at her. This was the Lori he knew. Falling into character in any situation was like breathing for her. He'd always had to work at it.

The receptionist hesitated, then surrendered. She handed a clipboard to Linc. "Have a seat and fill these out. I'll have Dr. Wall's assistant take you back for X-rays as soon as she can."

"Thank you." Linc was stunned. He'd expected to have to use his weapon.

"What's the name?" the receptionist asked.

"Lori Counts," he said quickly. Though he doubted Marcos would find them here, he wasn't taking any chances.

As they took seats he gave Lori a nod of approval for her performance, then he concentrated on filling out the forms with bogus personal info.

"Mrs. Counts."

He looked up at what had to be the dental assistant holding open the door that led back to the exam rooms. Linc stood, waited for Lori to go ahead of him. He hung on to the clipboard as the assistant guided them to a room and settled Lori into the chair.

"Mr. Counts, you'll need to wait in the corridor while I do the X-rays." She reached for the clipboard. "I'll take that for you."

"Sure." He gave up the forms and stepped outside the door.

The X-rays took about five minutes. The assistant

left the room briefly, then returned and hung the old-fashioned prints on the view box. She assured Lori that Dr. Wall would be with them soon.

Getting the dentist's cooperation wouldn't be quite so easy, but Linc now had a plan for that.

Twenty minutes later a guy, sixty or better, rushed into the room. "Sorry to keep you waiting." He offered a weary smile then settled on the stool next to Lori. "So you lost a crown, did you?" He pushed his glasses up the bridge of his nose.

Linc closed the door, and Dr. Wall looked up, startled. "We have a problem, doc." He pulled out his wallet, opened it slightly and flashed it far too quickly for the guy to see that there was no actual badge. "I'm U.S. Marshal Joe Duncan. This is a federal witness under my protection."

Wall blinked, still speechless. Whether it was fear or the thick lenses of his glasses, his eyes looked huge.

"We're staying at a safe house near here. I received notification from my superior that there is some question as to my witness's identity. To clear up the confusion I have digital copies of dental records I'd like you to compare to hers. Your assistance in this matter would be greatly appreciated. Time is very short and several lives are at stake."

The dentist looked stunned. "I... Of course I will

help." He stared at Lori a moment, then turned back to Linc. "I'll need the records."

"If you have internet access I can send them to your account."

Wall recited the office email address and notified his assistant to print them as soon as they arrived.

Linc attempted to put the dentist at ease. "I hope you realize how important your help is to this case. I can't thank you enough."

He nodded, a bit of a twinkle in his eyes now. "I watch *Law and Order.*"

The assistant was back in two minutes with the printout of Lori's dental records from before the explosion.

"All right." Wall spread the records on the small desk in the corner. He studied both sets at length.

Linc kept still though he wanted to pace, to climb the walls.

Finally Dr. Wall looked up. "This is difficult to call."

Linc moved closer to the desk. "How so?"

"The size of the jaw, the number and size of the teeth are exactly the same."

Anticipation had Linc's heart racing.

"There has been extensive cosmetic work since this older set was taken. Crowns, bridges and ve-neers. But neither shows any missing teeth or mal-formations to point to as unique to the patient." He shrugged. "There is no one particular item that would truly confirm the conclusion that both sets of X-rays belong to the same person." He pursed his lips. "I can say without reservation that both sets of records appear to be from the same individual, but I don't feel comfortable confirming that without a single unique trait." He shook his head. "I'm sorry, sir, but that's the best this old country dentist can do."

"You were a great deal of help, sir. Thank you." Linc walked to the door. Disappointment crushed against his chest. "I'll settle up with the lady at the front desk."

"Don't worry about the fee. I was no help, I fear." Wall pulled off his glasses. "But don't give up. There are those in the field who could make the identification for you. An expert with the kind of training and equipment I don't have."

"I'll bear that in mind. Thank you." Linc needed out of here. He couldn't breathe.

Lori quietly thanked Dr. Wall then walked out of the exam room behind Linc.

The receptionist smiled as they passed through the lobby. At the exit, Lori stalled.

Linc braced for trouble.

Lori looked back at the receptionist, who was busy with paperwork.

The seconds ticked off like gunshots in Linc's

head. He kept expecting her to demand that someone call the police.

Then she walked out the door.

Linc dragged in a breath and followed her out.

Lori didn't slow or look at him or even speak.

What was there to say? They knew nothing more than they had known before.

The dental records were a dead end for now.

Linc had no way of proving the truth to her beyond the shadow of a doubt.

At this point he would need a miracle to keep her cooperative. He'd stopped believing in miracles a long time ago.

His cell vibrated. He dragged it out and checked the screen. Keaton. With news about Marcos's arrival, Linc presumed. "Reece."

"We have a problem."

Linc didn't like the sound of that. "Go on."

"Lopez was not on the plane."

"Are you certain?"

"The Bureau just verified that Lopez and Marcos are one and the same. When the airfield was asked to verify the passengers who arrived, he was not among the three."

Linc didn't really hear what Keaton said next. All he could think was that Marcos could be anywhere.

He lowered the phone from his ear and surveyed the sidewalks and streets.

The bastard could be here.

Chapter Fourteen

Mia felt numb.

Dr. Wall hadn't been able to say for an absolute certainty that the dental records confirmed she was this Lori person, but he hadn't been able to conclude that she was not, either.

Same jawline, same number and size of teeth.

She glanced at the man looking around as if he didn't know what to do next. How could she be his wife and not know it? He was a total stranger to her…except for the feelings he evoked in her when they touched.

"We need transportation."

"Are we going back to the cabin?" She felt torn about that. The need to go home pulled at her. But where was home? Confusion rattled her brain.

"Maybe."

He took her hand and started forward. The jolt of sensation added to the confusing impulses already knocking around in her skull. She forced herself to analyze the feel of his skin against hers. Rougher than hers. Warm. Familiar. There it was again. His long fingers folded around hers made her feel safe. She shouldn't feel safe. What was wrong with her?

A run-down auto repair shop appeared to be his destination. He stopped to look at a red car that had seen better days. Reece let go of her hand and walked around the car, then leaned down and looked inside.

"Can I help you?"

Mia studied the man who'd joined them. Because of his grease-stained coveralls she assumed he was a mechanic. The smell of oil that lingered around him made her think of Teddy Stewart. He operated the mechanic shop in Blossom. The idea that he'd shown up at her house in the middle of the night toting that shotgun had her shaking her head. What had he been thinking? That Reece was dangerous, she acknowledged. Teddy had said he'd gotten his orders from her uncle. Why would Vince do that?

"She run good?" Reece asked, drawing Mia's attention back to the moment.

The mechanic nodded. "She don't look like much but she runs real good. Uses a little oil. I keep a bottle in the trunk."

Reece reached into his right front pocket and pulled out a thick fold of bills. "Six hundred work for you?" He counted off six one-hundred-dollar bills and handed them to the guy.

Who carried that kind of cash?

"That'll do." The mechanic reached inside the car and removed a document from the glove box. He signed the back and handed it to Reece. "That's the title. Keys are in the ignition."

That easily, they had transportation.

A minute or two later they were driving away. The upholstery was soiled and threadbare, but the car ran and rode smoothly enough.

"You hungry?"

Mia hadn't thought of food since the previous evening. "Maybe." Her stomach actually felt queasy. "I don't know."

"I'll pick up something at that first convenience store we passed." He glanced at the dash. "And fuel."

Mia didn't care either way. In an effort to relax she tried to study the old homes that lined the street as they drove through town, but questions kept intruding on her mind. She refused to entertain them. They were too overwhelming.

Reece slowed and turned into the convenience store drive. He pulled up to the gas pumps and shut off the engine.

"You want to go in?"

Mia shook her head and closed her eyes. She just wanted to hide. To curl up in a fetal position.

He hesitated but finally gave up and went inside. She understood that he was afraid she'd make a run for it. The thought had crossed her mind back at the dental office. For a moment she'd struggled with the impulse to ask the receptionist to call the police. To end this here and now. But she couldn't do it. How insane was that?

Mia opened her eyes and sought the man who had yanked the rug from under her feet. Reece looked toward the car several times as he waited at the counter inside the store. She felt sorry for him. He desperately wanted to prove his wife was alive and to have her back.

He'd suffered just as Mia had.

The limp was more obvious as he walked back to the car. The workout getting to town on foot had been hard on him. She'd been so numb and disoriented she'd scarcely paid attention to the physical effort required.

He thrust a bag through the driver's window. She took it and peeked at the contents while he pumped the gas. Chicken and fries and soft drinks. The smell of the fried foods had her appetite stirring. Maybe she could eat. Undoubtedly, she should.

Reece slid behind the steering wheel and started the car. He didn't say anything as he drove away from the convenience store and headed toward the narrow, crooked road where their hideout waited. How could this be happening to her?

Mia wanted to blast him for turning her world upside down. What he was suggesting negated all that she had achieved in seven years—her entire life, for all intents and purposes. Reece had the memories of his wife. He had his life dating back to the day he was born. Why couldn't that be enough? Why did he have to take hers?

The answer to that question pressed down on her shoulders, expanded in her chest. Because if what he alleged was true, Mia's life was not real. It was fiction. Like the stories mothers read to their children before bedtime.

She stared at the blur of trees outside her window. For seven years she had been Mia Marie Grant. Daughter of William and Freda Grant. Graduate of Boulder High School. Plaster artisan and happy-go-lucky friend and neighbor of folks in Blossom. She was poor Mia who had cheated death and been reborn.

But what if she wasn't Mia Grant? She sneaked a glimpse of the man driving. What if she was his long-lost wife? What if the life she'd had before her accident had been full and happy? Restoring a home together. Fighting crime together. Had Vincent

Lopez, or whoever Reece claimed her uncle was, really cheated Reece and his wife out of that life?

"Why didn't you have children?"

Reece glanced at her. He turned his attention back to the road just as quickly. "We had a plan."

The shaking started again, deep inside Mia. It had been happening all day. "Tell me about your plan." She needed to know, though the reason eluded her. The whole concept was as self-defeating as throwing salt on an open wound, but like a passerby staring at the scene of a five-car pileup, she had to see...to know.

"Our five-year plan." His profile hardened with the grim words. "The first three were focused on finding a home in a good neighborhood for raising kids. Settling in." His shoulder lifted and fell as if the whole story was irrelevant. "Then we'd start a family. No more undercover work for...her."

They would have children by now. The reality hit Mia harder than anything else she'd heard today. She had wondered about children. Would she ever have any? Would she ever even find love? The accident had set all her hopes and dreams back by a decade. With her uncle's protective hovering she might never have any of that. She wanted those things...she had dreamed of being in love.

"Do you still have the house?" Mia hoped he had

kept the house. It had meant so much to his wife, and they'd worked so hard to restore it.

Reece made the turn onto the narrow drive that led up to the cabin. "I put it on the market right before I left L.A."

Mia held her breath as he turned the car around so that he could back it up next to the far end of the cabin, out of sight.

He shoved the gearshift into Park and shut off the engine. "Got an offer two weeks later." He dropped his hands onto his thighs. "But I couldn't do it. I had the Realtor close it up. We'd paid for it with the savings she had from her parents' estate. It wasn't mine to sell."

The relief she felt was unreasonable. She shouldn't be feeling any of this. Mia climbed out of the car, holding the bag of food that now turned her stomach, and walked away. She shouldn't have asked those questions. The answers made her hurt.

Reece moved around her slow steps, striding quickly to the cabin. By the time she reached the porch he was inside. She entered, dropped the sack on the table and reached for one of the soft drinks. She could use the caffeine and the sugar.

And the truth. That was what she really needed.

Could her uncle confirm what she believed to be her past? A simple trip to Boulder would do the trick. But she'd never known she needed to look for confirmation.

"You should eat."

She set the soft drink down and faced him. "How did you do it? Keep going afterward, I mean."

He stood only three or four feet away but it felt like he was pressed against her. The urge to be closer, to hold him and make this right somehow felt as urgent as the need to breathe.

For what felt like an eternity he looked at her. His eyes, so blue, so intense, made her ache to know every thought and hope behind them.

"I took the most dangerous assignments in hopes that I'd find myself on the wrong end of a discharged weapon since I didn't have the guts to do it myself."

Emotion twisted in her chest. "You wanted to die?"

"Every day. Breakfast included a shot of bourbon and the business end of my weapon." He opened his soda and downed a long gulp, then shrugged. "Then one day I stopped."

The trembling extended outward. She wrapped her arms around her middle to hide the quaking. "When did you stop?"

He leveled a gaze on her that weakened her knees. "When I found you."

Mia dropped into the closest chair. Her legs

couldn't hold her another second. She wet her lips. "You're that certain?"

"Yes." He braced his hands on the back of a chair at the table. "The FBI has confirmed that Vincent Lopez and Juan Marcos are one and the same. I got the call a few minutes ago."

Outside the dental clinic. She remembered. Weariness weighed down on her, threatening to drag her into unconsciousness. At least this time she wasn't seeing spots.

What did all this mean? Other than the minor changes prompted by the surgeries, he claimed she looked exactly like his wife. The dental records were practically identical, though the small-town dentist hadn't wanted to make the call. Her unexpected skill at repairing historic plaster had come about in the same manner as his wife's. They shared a love for historic homes. Her uncle appeared to be the criminal Reece asserted he was. The photos her uncle had declared were Mia were in fact Reece's wife.

But the most glaring aspect for Mia was the reaction she experienced each time they touched. One of the specialists she'd seen had suggested there was actually an explanation for her moments of déjà vu and sensations of familiarity with certain scents and touches. He insisted that her suddenly found plaster restoration skill fell into the same category.

Sensory and muscle memory.

She may have lost the memories of her life before but her fingers, her hands remembered the movements associated with reforming damaged plaster. That had seemed ridiculous to her at the time, since the past she had been given didn't include historic homes or anything related to them. The other part, however, she had accepted. Certain smells, certain things she touched were forever ingrained in her senses.

Learning that Reece's wife had restored plaster seemed to confirm the specialist's opinion.

The only answer was glaringly obvious.

She was Lori Reece.

She grabbed for courage and did the only thing she could. "Do you have a picture?"

He exhaled a heavy breath. "Too much has happened today. We should take a break." He stared down at his hands, braced on the chair. "We shouldn't have gone this far. It could be bad for you."

Both their lives were hanging in the balance and he was worried about this exchange being bad for her? A surge of adrenaline fired through her and she launched to her feet. "The accident—car crash or explosion—was bad for me! Losing my whole history, whichever one it was, was bad for me! But neither of those things killed me. I don't think trying to find the truth will, either." She dragged in a ragged breath, telling herself to calm down, that going off like this would accomplish nothing.

His gaze bored into hers with such ferocity that she caught her breath. "The man you have believed is your uncle may very well kill you if he discovers you know the truth."

Mia stormed across the room to where he stood. "Do you have a photo or not?"

For three frantic pounds of her heart she was certain he would refuse her. Then he reached for his wallet. The leather was worn soft, its black color faded to gray around the edges. He'd carried it for a while. Inside was more cash, a driver's license and a few small folded papers. He fingered beneath an inner flap and pulled out a photo. He handed it to her.

Mia reclaimed her seat. The back of the photo read "Catalina" and the date. Carefully, she turned over the photo and peered at the couple pictured there.

Reece looked young and happy. His face bore no trace of the grim lines he wore now or the scar. The woman, Lori, smiled as if this were the happiest day of her life. Her eyes…her lips were…Mia's. The hair, even the way she parted it, was Mia's. The shape of her face…the line of her jaw.

Mia sucked in a breath. Her hand went to her

mouth to trace the lips reflected in the photo. This could be her.

She really could be Lori Reece…his wife.

Oh, my God. She looked up. "You've been carrying this photo all this time?"

"I stopped taking it out and looking at it a long time ago but I couldn't bring myself to store it away. That was taken on our honeymoon on Catalina Island. We were too busy to take a real honeymoon so we just went away for the weekend." He laughed, the sound painful to hear. "Turned out to be the best weekend…" He pushed away from the chair. "I should check things outside."

Mia didn't ask him any more questions. She wasn't the only one this was bad for. She stared at the photo. If all this was true, how did she stop being Mia Grant and start being Lori Reece?

If this had been her life, why had it been taken from her?

12:50 p.m.

LINC COULDN'T QUIET the thundering in his chest.

He scanned the tree line, listened for traffic in the distance. The quiet was endless…except for the storm inside him.

Safeguarding Lori was his main objective right now and he couldn't begin to focus on the necessary steps. Marcos could be anywhere. The chances of him finding them here were nominal at best. What troubled Linc the most was that Marcos might have gone underground. He had succeeded in evading detection by law enforcement for seven years already. Linc wanted him behind bars for the rest of his life. Or dead, which was preferable.

That was something he would have to deal with soon. Time was an enemy. Marcos would protect himself first and foremost. That he never gave up anything that belonged to him without a fight could prove his downfall this time. Linc knew his M.O. by heart now. For whatever reason, Marcos had taken Lori and claimed her as his own. He would exhaust every means available to him to get her back, as long as his freedom was not in jeopardy.

That was a reality Linc would have to deal with, but not today. Today he had to make sure Lori was handling the truth. Strangely, she seemed to be dealing with it better than he was. Mostly because of the uncertainty factor. Just because she accepted the truth about who she was didn't mean she would accept him.

That, he wasn't sure he could deal with.

He walked back inside. She stood in the middle of the room. As soon as his gaze met hers she held out the photo to him.

"I have more questions for you."

He accepted the photo and tucked it back into his wallet. "You can ask me anything."

She squared her shoulders as if what she was about to ask took a great deal of courage. "I've been on a few dates since…the accident. Been kissed a couple of times but nothing more."

Jealousy roared but he kept his mouth shut.

"No one has made me react to the sense of touch the way you do." She looked away. "There's no possibility I'll ever get my memory back, but one of the specialists I saw suggested that sensory or muscle memory could be the explanation for those déjà vu moments I have occasionally."

His throat tightened. "You have those with me?"

She nodded. "When you hold my hand or stand close to me I feel safe." Her gaze met his. "Like when you've been away and then you come home."

Linc scrubbed his hand over his face, blinked at the sting in his eyes. He had cried once in his life… when he'd had to admit defeat in the search for her. He hadn't succumbed to the urge since…until now.

"Your wife—"

"Lori." She needed to get used to that.

"There must have been special ways you touched her or kissed her that she liked most." Her cheeks flamed red as she spoke. "I thought maybe that would help me feel something from…before."

The storm inside him stilled. "You want me to show you."

She nodded. "Yes." Her chest rose and fell with a shaky breath. "I need to feel this. The pieces are falling together in my brain, but I need the cement to hold them there."

Linc took a step toward her and saw her shiver. "Lori liked when we sat on the sofa and just watched TV. We didn't get to do a lot of that, but she loved cuddling." Safe enough place to start.

She moved to the sofa and sat down, her posture still rigid, those golden-brown eyes watching him expectantly. He sat down beside her. His nerves jangled. Damn. He was nervous as hell. That hadn't happened since the night he'd asked her to marry him.

"Now what?" she asked when he made no other move.

Linc draped his arm around her shoulder. "We just sort of got close and hugged up."

She turned toward him, leaned her head on his shoulder, her hands on his chest, causing his heart to squeeze. His fingers found their way to her hair. He'd been aching to touch those silky tresses. Closing his eyes, he savored the feel of her against him. The sweet smell of her hair. He rested his other hand on her arm, caressed her soft skin.

She inhaled deeply as if she wanted to draw in

his scent. Another of her little shivers created a new friction everywhere their bodies touched.

They sat that way for a long while. She melted against him and he absorbed her heat, his whole body hungry for any taste of her.

Eventually, she raised her head and turned her face to his. "I don't understand how I can have no memory of you and yet I feel like I belong this way... in your arms."

The admission got to him on a level nothing had touched since the day he'd lost her. Linc couldn't take much more. "May I kiss you?" If he died tomorrow, having kissed Lori again would make his death worthwhile.

She stared at his lips a moment, then she tilted her mouth toward his. The soft fullness of her mouth was as familiar as his own name. He cupped her face and kissed her slowly, thoroughly. The way Lori liked to be kissed. Her fingers threaded into his hair and she kissed him back. She kissed the way she lived. Wild and sweet, relentless. As if tomorrow would never come and she had to do it all today. He lowered her down onto the ragged sofa and lost himself in the kiss.

Her hands went under his shirt and she shook hard as her palms flowed over his skin. His entire body reacted. He wanted to do the same to her but he had to maintain some sense of control. He was hard as a rock and she was moving under him, making him want all of her.

Linc moved onto his knees on the floor. She made a sound of disapproval. Her lids fluttered open and there was his Lori, all flushed and wanting.

He smiled. "This is an old favorite." He leaned forward and kissed the tip of her nose, then her chin and down her throat until he encountered her T-shirt. When his lips stopped moving, she gasped. He stared at the T-shirt a moment with the understanding that going there might be a no-turning-back move.

Before he could convince himself to back off, she took the decision out of his hands. She grabbed the hem of her T-shirt and slid it up and off.

Her breasts were as beautiful as he remembered. Perfect. Firm. He squeezed his fingers into fists to prevent touching her. This was not about what he wanted. This had to be about what she wanted. What Lori had loved. He continued that path from the base of her throat to her breasts. She trembled and arched her back to show she wanted more.

He leaned close to her ear and whispered, "This is what you loved me to do to your breasts." When his mouth closed over one taut nipple, she gasped. Linc remembered every detail of what Lori loved, of the soft sounds she made. The gentle kisses, the lavish attention with his tongue, and the way he suckled each breast until the building tension had her screaming his name.

Her fingers dug into his hair and she pulled his face up to hers. "Linc, just do it! I can't take any more!"

He drew away, dropped back onto his heels. His hands shook. His entire body pulsed with the need to be inside her. This was the way his wife had always let him know to get down to business. He searched her desire-glazed eyes. Had she remembered? "Lori?"

Her lips quivered. She made a frantic sound as one arm went over her breasts and she grabbed for her shirt with the other. She scrambled away from him and dragged on the top.

He'd gone too far. Linc pushed to his feet and dragged a hand through his hair. "I'm sorry. I shouldn't have let that happen."

"Don't you understand?" she cried.

Linc dared to face her. He deserved whatever she tossed at him. He'd gone too damned far.

She flung out her arms. "You made me feel things! Like I was where I'd always belonged." She shook her head. "It's some kind of bond that's real and I felt it." Hot tears flowed down her cheeks, and she swiped at them with both hands. "I believe you, okay? I'm not Mia Grant. God only knows what kind of monster my supposed uncle is."

"We'll work this out," Linc promised. "We'll find the right doctors. We'll do whatever we have to."

She shook her head. "That's not the problem. The trouble is you want her back. I can't be her." A sob burst from her lips. "She's gone and I can't bring her back for you."

Chapter Fifteen

Mia couldn't take any more.

Her body still shook with the emotions and sensations he had aroused inside her. She had wanted more of him so badly...had sensed that making love with him would be a natural progression. She had no memory of making love, of how it felt to experience an orgasm. No matter, she felt certain that the shimmering, building sensations that had bombarded her moments ago had been headed toward that place.

But none of it had been for her—the woman she was now. It had been for Lori. The woman who knew to call him Linc and who knew just the right moment to urge him to fill her completely.

The sweet, warm glow he had kindled inside her had been abruptly extinguished. That life, those memories, had been stolen from her. Fury started to build. She wanted to hear Vincent Lopez—or Juan Marcos—admit the truth. She wanted him to tell her to her face that he had taken her whole life away from her under the guise of kindness and loyalty to her father—a man that he had never even known. A man she had no memory of because all that she had been was erased.

"You don't have to be her."

Mia whirled to face Reece. The desolation on his face made her ache.

He moved his head from side to side. "What you do with your life is your decision. I can't make that decision for you. But don't expect me to stop loving my wife just because you can't be that person anymore."

He still loved her. That choking sensation she'd suffered recently tightened her throat, and emotion burned her eyes. No matter what he said, he wanted their life back. He wanted his wife back.

She summoned her determination. What she had to do was clear. "I want to go back."

The desolation was joined by a new misery. "Going back to your life in Blossom won't be safe until Marcos is apprehended."

"I'm not asking you to take me back to my life there." She pushed aside the fear that threatened to undermine her fortitude. "I want to confront the man who did this." What she really wanted was to watch him suffer as she had…as she would in the weeks, months and possibly years to come.

Reece shook his head. "It's too dangerous. We stay right here until the feds get the situation under control. At the moment we don't know for certain where he is."

"I can find him."

Reece's face cleared of emotion. "How?"

"He gave me a number to call if I ever needed him when he was away. All I have to do is call." The plan instantly solidified in her brain. "I'll tell him that this crazy man kidnapped me and I need help."

"He won't go for that."

A disgusted smile toyed with her lips. "He will. If he told me once, he's told me a thousand times. I'm the daughter he always wanted. I gave him a reason to live."

"Marcos never married," Reece countered. "Word was he preferred no ties."

"I think maybe you got the wrong word." She cocked her head and eyed him with complete confidence. "Family is very important to him. By the time he learned of the existence of extended family in Blossom, they were gone, except for Gloria. Gloria and I are all he has."

"Even if your plan would work, it's far too dangerous." Reece stubbornly held his ground.

"Maybe for you." She held hers, as well. "But I'm going to end this with or without you."

Southern Medical Center, Winchester, Tennessee, 7:15 p.m.

LINC DIDN'T LIKE THIS one little bit.

Keaton, having flown in, had taken a position outside the hospital with two FBI agents from Nashville. Dressed in scrubs, Linc and two additional Bureau agents had assumed positions in the E.R.

Lori was taking a hell of a risk. Linc hadn't been able to stop her and he'd damned sure tried, all the way up until the time she'd made the call an hour ago. Keaton and Jim Colby from the Colby Agency had coordinated with the Bureau. Linc was stunned at how quickly the operation had come together. Just showed how badly the Bureau wanted Marcos. That the Nashville office would take down such a high-profile international criminal was all the incentive the agents had needed. The Franklin County Sheriff's Department was recovering Linc's SUV, ensuring the report was broadcast wide on their police channels. If Marcos had eyes and ears in local law enforcement, he would only hear about the accident and transport of two victims to the nearby Winchester hospital. The operation inside the hospital was off the books as far as local law enforcement went.

All involved with the op were linked with wireless communications. Posted at the nurse's station, Linc had a visual on Lori in the examination room, thanks to a monitor. On it, he saw her lying in the bed fidgeting with the sheet. He was less than twelve yards away from her room, could see the doorway, and still Linc didn't like it.

Lori had made the call in character as the victim of a man who had apparently lost his mind. Linc felt as if he were losing his right now. If anything went wrong...

He'd given her his weapon. He knew the Beretta wouldn't fail her—if she remembered how to use it. He'd given her some instruction before they'd left the cabin, but she couldn't hit the broad side of a barn. Apparently her shooting skills had been lost along with her memories of their life together.

As he watched her, every ounce of willpower he possessed was required to keep his mind off those hot, mindless minutes on the sofa. He hoped that wouldn't be the last chance he'd get to make love to her. But he couldn't push her. Just because she had loved him before didn't mean she would ever love him again. That possibility tore at his heart. He didn't want to lose her again.

He wanted her back, but more than that, he wanted her safe and happy. He could live with whatever her decision was as long as she was alive and well.

He touched her image on the monitor. Her dark hair spread over the white pillow made him smile. He'd loved waking up with her lying beside him.

He would give anything to have her back like that. Anything.

"We have an arrival." Keaton's voice echoed across the communications link. "Latina matching the description of Gloria Lopez."

"That's it?" Linc had known this wouldn't go down so easily. Marcos was too cagey to fall into a trap like this. The feds had recognized that the same as Linc had. A separate operation was in place at Marcos's Blossom mansion. If Marcos went there, thinking the heat was here, he had a surprise coming.

"That's it," Keaton confirmed. "She's coming in through the E.R. entrance."

Linc was stopping this right now. "This is over."

"No."

The announcement came from Lori.

"The risk is pointless if Marcos is a no-show," Linc argued. Frustration growled inside him. He started around the counter and had to turn back as Gloria Lopez swept through the double doors leading from the lobby.

"Back off, Reece," Lori warned, sounding like the cop she'd once been.

"Heads up," he murmured back. "She's on her way in."

"Where is my niece?" Gloria demanded of the

nurse, who was also a federal agent, at the counter. "They told me up front that she's back here."

Linc kept his back turned. He thumbed through a chart.

"What's your niece's name, ma'am?"

"Mia Grant."

"Exam room four. We're waiting for a report on her X-rays."

"Thank you."

Linc turned around as Gloria Lopez entered Lori's room. He shook his head, fury starting to pound at his skull. This was a mistake.

Gloria rushed to Lori's bedside and hugged her. The dramatic gushing made Linc sick to his stomach. The woman acted as if she genuinely loved Lori. Lori played the terrified survivor flawlessly. When she asked about her uncle, Gloria explained that his plane had been delayed but that he would arrive soon.

Linc wasn't buying it.

He watched the monitor, tension building. Was Marcos coming? Gloria kept assuring Lori that he was. When Gloria asked about Reece, Lori gave her the planned answer. He had been knocked unconscious in the accident. Once he'd been taken away in the ambulance she didn't know what had happened to him.

Gloria got comfortable in a side chair and dropped

her bag at her feet as if she was in no hurry and actually was waiting for her supposed brother-in-law's arrival.

Linc listened closely to the conversation. This didn't feel right. Why would Marcos send a sacrificial lamb? Linc had fully expected he wouldn't show up, but sending a woman in his stead didn't fit the Marcos profile.

"This is wrong," he spat out.

MIA FLINCHED AT REECE's harshly spoken words.

"Are you in pain, sweetie?" Gloria leaned toward Mia and patted her arm. "Do you want me to call someone?"

Mia manufactured a smile. "I'm okay. Just the occasional twinge." She rubbed her shoulder. "The seat belt did a number on me."

Gloria sighed. "I can't believe this happened. Not after what you've been through already. It's just awful."

Mia worried that Reece was right. Her faux uncle wasn't going to show. Gloria would probably get a call any second now saying as much. "I'm okay." She managed a more genuine smile. "Now that you're here."

"Oh." She took Mia's hand. "My butterfly. I couldn't bear it if anything happened to you." She sighed. "Vinny is beside himself."

"You should call him and let him know I'm okay. Or let me talk to him. I tried to explain to his assistant that I was all right but I'm not sure the message was passed along properly." If he was close, the number could be traced to his position...maybe. She couldn't remember how that worked exactly, but surely she'd done that when she was a cop.

She stilled. Had she just thought of herself as Lori Reece? She shook herself mentally and chalked it up to the staggering events of the day.

"...been delayed. I'm sure he'll catch up with us by the time we're home."

Mia cleared her head. "I'm sorry, what?" She had to pay attention. She resisted the need to adjust the weapon Reece had given her. It had slipped farther down her thighs. Still within reach, she hoped.

Gloria patted Mia's hand. "Don't worry, your uncle will be here soon. Even if he's been delayed he'll see you at home."

That would not work. "I'm not sure when they're going to release me," Mia said, as much for those listening via the communications as for Gloria. "We may be here awhile."

"I hope they've arrested that terrible man," Gloria offered with a shake of her head. "Why in the world would he do this?" She turned a worried face to Mia. "And you thought he was so nice."

Mia suddenly understood what she needed to do.

"He said some things...." A sharp "no" from Reece hissed across the com link.

"What kind of things?" Gloria's concern appeared authentic.

Mia pushed away the confusion. Now was not a good time to analyze that aspect of this bizarre relationship. "That my name wasn't Mia Grant and that you and Vince had lied to me all these years."

Horror claimed Gloria's face. She gasped. "Is he insane? Where did he come from? What was he doing in Blossom?"

"He's from Los Angeles." Mia bit her lip and frowned as if struggling to recall all that Reece had said. "He said that I'm his wife."

Reece swore in her ear.

"That's just crazy," Gloria wailed. But her face told a different story. The softer emotions vanished, and suspicion and anger took their place. "Your uncle will be so alarmed. With your condition, that sort of nonsense is the last thing you need." She swung her head from side to side. "This is just awful."

"What's worse," Mia pressed, "is he kept saying he was taking me to the police. I hope he didn't regain consciousness and start spouting that crazy talk." She rubbed her forehead and tried to look worried. "What if they won't let me go home?" The uncle Mia knew would not delay coming to her rescue. He had always done exactly that, even when she hadn't wanted him to.

"Oh, Lord." Gloria launched to her feet. "We should call him."

That was what Mia had been hoping for. "I think that's a good idea."

Gloria snatched up her purse. "First we should get out of this excuse for a hospital." She literally shimmied with urgency. "Your uncle will take care of this, but first I should get you safely home. You should be under the care of your own doctors."

Not the reaction Mia had hoped for. Real worry yanked at her nerves. "Gloria, you know I can't go until they release me."

Gloria walked to the door and peeked out. "They're probably just keeping you here under false pretenses," she whispered to Mia, "until the police can investigate his claims." She made an angry sound, a growl almost, as she strode back to the bed. "That awful man is trying to take you away from us."

Worry shifted to apprehension. "I think he's just delusional." Mia had never seen her aunt behave this way. "The hospital wouldn't keep me unless it was medically necessary." Reece growled a caution in her ear, the tone every bit as ferocious as Gloria's.

Gloria's face pinched with anger. "You just don't know what people are capable of. We've always shielded you from these unsavory goings-on. Now, come along." She ushered Mia to climb out of the bed. "We're leaving this incompetent place."

Mia let the gun slip down to the mattress before swinging her legs over the edge. "I think you're overreacting." She tucked a handful of hair behind her ear, adopting an expression of regret. "I shouldn't have told you." Mia had to do some serious backtracking. "None of what he said matters. We'll go home as soon as Uncle Vincent gets here."

Gloria grabbed her by the arm, her fingers biting into Mia's skin. "We have to go now."

"I'm coming in," was muttered in Mia's ear.

"No," she fairly shouted. She glanced at the hidden camera, hoping to stall Reece. "Gloria, you need to calm down. He'll be here soon and you'll have gotten all worked up for nothing."

"I won't let them take you from me." She tugged more insistently on Mia's arm. "Come along. We have to hurry."

"I… My clothes. I need my clothes." It was the only stall tactic Mia had left.

Reluctantly, Gloria released Mia and snatched the jeans and T-shirt slung over the back of the chair. "Hurry."

Mia took her time dragging on the jeans. Gloria paced like a caged animal, her impatience visibly mounting. Mia turned her back to the camera before removing the hospital gown. Reece had already seen her naked from the waist up but she wasn't ready for that to happen again. Uncertainty and a hint of humiliation already nagged at her. She pulled on the shirt and stepped into her shoes.

"You're going too slow." Gloria grabbed her arm again. "Let's go."

"You know they'll try to stop us," Mia reminded her in a last-ditch effort to make her think rationally.

Gloria dug into the purse slung over her shoulder. "They're not going to take you away from me." She pulled out a small handgun. "I won't let that happen."

The air rushed out of Mia's lungs. "Oh, my God."

"I have to protect you," Gloria insisted, the gun held loosely in her right hand as if she weren't sure of precisely how to hold it. "Your uncle would never forgive me if I didn't."

This couldn't be happening. Gloria hand-fed dogs, rocked them like children. She loved all things. She wouldn't hurt a fly. "Please put the gun away. You're not thinking clearly." Mia shouldn't have pushed the situation. What had she done? "Please, Gloria."

Reece burst through the door before Mia finished the plea. "Put down the gun!" His weapon was leveled and aimed at Gloria.

"No!" This was Mia's fault. She'd caused this!

Gloria glared at Reece. "You!" She pointed her gun at him. "You won't take her away from me."

"Put down the gun," Reece warned, "or I will shoot."

Gloria's face contorted with fury. She tightened her hold on Mia's arm. "Let's go. Ignore him. He's not going to shoot. He wouldn't dare risk hitting you."

Mia stared at the woman, dumbfounded. "Don't do this, Gloria."

"Do as I say, Mia." She glowered at Reece. "He's just a sad, pathetic man who should have died seven years ago."

Mia shook loose from her vicious clutch. "What're you saying?" How did Gloria know Reece? Why would she think he should have died seven years ago? The voice of truth screamed in Mia's head.

"That doesn't matter right now, Butterfly." She motioned for Mia to come to her, her aim at Reece never deviating from center chest. "Let's hurry. He just wants to tear us apart."

"By telling me the truth?" Fury battered Mia as the whole truth assimilated in her brain. Gloria had helped build this nightmare. She was equally responsible for stealing Mia's life.

"Come," Gloria commanded, her face twisted with menace, "or I'll shoot him."

Mia quieted the fury raging inside her. She nodded, the movement stiff. "Whatever you say, Gloria."

The instant Gloria's full attention swung back to Reece, Mia shoved her hand beneath the sheet and seized the gun. She grasped it with both hands as she turned the barrel on the woman who had bathed her when she could not bathe herself. The woman who had fed her when she could not feed herself. The woman who had lied to her and stolen her life.

"Shoot him and I swear I will shoot you." Mia's heart raged against her breastbone.

"Mia...you're my sweetheart...my precious butterfly," Gloria implored. "You wouldn't hurt me."

Reece rushed her. He disarmed Gloria before Mia could blink. The weapon slipped from Mia's hands and clattered on the tile floor.

The other agents streamed into the room. Gloria screamed and howled as they subdued her and read her the Miranda rights.

Mia couldn't move. Shock, she decided. She was in shock.

There was no longer any doubt.

She was Lori Reece.

Her gaze sifted through the tangle of activity around her, coming to rest on the man attempting to cut through the chaos to get to her.

Her husband.

Chapter Sixteen

Nashville Federal Holding Facility, 11:15 p.m.

Mia watched the man she had known as her uncle
for the past seven years. On the other side of the
viewing glass he sat, shackled, at a small table. The
interview room was generic white. Only the table
and two folding chairs held court in the middle of
the austere space. Nothing about it was designed
for comfort.

"They've been pushing him for two hours," the
special agent in charge said. "He isn't talking."

Reece stared in disgust at the man who had dev-
astated his life. "He won't talk."

Mia glanced at Reece but she couldn't meet his
gaze. After Gloria had been taken away, Keaton had
driven Mia and Reece here. Marcos had been trans-
ported to this location after his capture in Blossom.
As Reese had suspected, Marcos had felt confident

returning to Blossom, since Mia and Reece were in Winchester. He had departed from and arrived at alternative airfields while a decoy plane took the expected route in order to throw off any surveillance. The agents had been smart to move quickly. Marcos had only returned to clear out his safe room, a room Mia hadn't known existed.

After his capture the Bureau had contacted DEA, who suspected that Marcos had been using his art and antiques business as well as massive nursery shipments across the country for transporting drugs. The Colombian government, with new drug laws in place, was happy to cooperate in his prosecution. His property there was being searched at this very hour.

All of it had happened so fast. Mia felt weak and disoriented. As confused as she felt, there was one thing she had to do before moving forward into the unknown. "I have to talk to him." She turned to the special agent, who didn't attempt to hide his surprise.

"Miss Grant," Agent Krober said with obvious skepticism, "I understand the compulsion you feel to ask him certain questions. But—"

"I'm sorry, Agent Krober, but you couldn't possibly understand. I have to talk to him." She felt Reece watching her but Mia couldn't look at him. "I just have to."

Krober exchanged a look with Reece. He nodded once, then turned back to the viewing window.

Her request hurt him, she knew. Mia regretted that, more than words could adequately articulate, but this was something she had to do.

"All right. Five minutes, Miss Grant." Krober led the way out of the room. "Do not discuss any aspect of his business operation."

Reece kept his back turned as Mia followed the agent. Her heart rammed harder and harder against her breastbone. Uncertainty, pain, regret and anger had combined inside her, creating a tornado that wouldn't allow her to hold on to her equilibrium.

She wanted this nightmare over.

But this part couldn't be skipped.

Krober opened the door to the interview room. Mia took a deep breath and stepped inside. The shackled man she refused to call her uncle observed her closely as she crossed to the table. Mia sat down, facing him. It wasn't until she looked into his eyes, eyes that had shown such love and care for her, that hatred ignited inside her.

"Why?" That was the only answer she wanted. Then she never wanted to hear his voice again. Never wanted to see him or receive any news of him.

He didn't speak, just continued staring at her.

The blazing hatred exploded into hot tendrils of

fury. She slammed her palms on the table. "Why did you do this to me?"

He laughed, a dry, hostile sound. "Why what? Why did I ensure you received world-class medical care? Why did I ensure your complete recovery from a tragic accident? Or why did I put you in the loving hands of my sister-in-law, who treated you like her own child?"

Mia shook with a new bombardment of blistering emotion. "You stole my life." Her voice ached with the misery that would not be overshadowed by her rage. He had taken everything from her. Even her name.

He leaned forward. "Your life was over. You were dying." His face twisted with fury of his own. "I saved you and this is how you repay me."

Mia struggled to maintain her composure. "Say it." She swallowed to ease the choking sensation deep in her throat. "I want to hear you say my real name." She needed him to confirm the truth screaming for attention inside her. She wanted to hear the words. "Say it."

He smirked. "You know your name."

"Say it!"

A smile slid across his evil lips. "You are Mia Grant, daughter of—"

"Stop lying." She rocketed to her feet and the chair

screeched across the tile floor. "My real name. The one you robbed me of."

He lifted his gaze to hers. "Whatever stories they tell you, Butterfly, your name has always been and will always be Mia Grant. You are not who they say you are. And they cannot prove their allegations."

"You son of a bitch."

"Your father would be ashamed of you." The bastard shook his head. "Reece has done this to you."

"You," she blasted him, "did this to me."

Another of those malicious smiles spread across his face. "Prove it."

"I will find the whole truth if I have to retrace every step you took seven years ago."

He laughed. "You will never know for certain. That is the gift I leave you with."

If she'd had a gun she would have killed him. The need throbbed in her very soul. But she would not. A sense of victory calmed her. He didn't deserve to die quickly. She wanted him to rot in prison, slowly and surely.

Mia turned her back on him and walked out. She braced against the wall in the corridor, and no longer able to hold back her emotion, she let the tears flow.

She squeezed her eyes shut against the pain. He was lying. She understood this with complete certainty, but she'd needed to hear him say the words. And he had robbed her of that, too.

Her eyes opened and lit on Reece, who waited a few feet away. Dear God, what did she do now? He would want answers of his own. How could she blame him?

She wasn't Mia Grant but she wasn't Lori Reece, either. The memories of her life before the explosion were gone. The ones she had made since were irrelevant.

She was no one.

"This is…overwhelming. I know." He shoved his hands into the pockets of his jeans.

He looked so incredibly sad, her heart grieved for him. "It's…" She shook her head. There were no words to describe how she felt. "I can't explain."

"Tell me what you want me to do." He dared to draw another step nearer. "Whatever it is, I'll do it."

He wanted to help. He wanted his wife back. Wanted his life the way it used to be. But she couldn't give him those things.

"I need time." She hauled in a heavy breath. "I have to figure this out."

He reached into his pocket and withdrew a piece of paper. "The Colby Agency says this place is the best on the planet for recoveries from…things like this." He offered the paper to her.

She took it, careful not to touch his outstretched fingers. Dealing with her reactions to his touch was more than she could endure just now. "Thank you." She tucked the paper into her pocket.

"Where will you go?"

The hurt in his voice ripped at her heart. But it was the single tear that slid down his unshaven jaw that shredded her composure completely. She had to hold him. Stepping forward, she put her arms around him and rested her head against his chest. He shook with his own emotional struggle as he hugged her tight. Listening to the pounding of his heart and inhaling the scent that was uniquely his chased away the fear and anguish.

She felt safe.

They held each other that way for a long time.

Mia hated to release him but it was time to go.

The only way to begin her life again was to go away for a while and sort through these debilitating emotions. When she was strong enough she would make the hard decisions.

Pulling back, her soul grieved the loss. She wiped her eyes and reached for courage. "I have a lot to fix." She almost laughed. Was that even possible? He'd used that word. "So I do have to go." She drew in a resolute breath. "I just don't know exactly where and for how long."

"I understand. You do what you have to." That

vivid blue gaze held hers with a compassion that had more tears brimming in her eyes. "Wherever you go, know that I'll be waiting. For as long as it takes."

She nodded, then turned away before she broke down completely. Leaving him standing there, watching her go, was the hardest thing she'd ever had to do.

Chapter Seventeen

Chicago, Friday, July 1, 9:00 p.m.

Hazel's was packed. Among the throng, Linc waved to the bartender for another round. Nearly forty-eight hours and he hadn't heard from Lori. He shouldn't have hoped to, much less expected to. Evidently, he was human after all.

The bartender delivered the triple shot of bourbon and Linc knocked it back. That was enough. Walking those three blocks home was still possible. Barely.

"You're getting soft, Reece."

Linc looked up to find his former boss climbing onto the stool next to him. He placed a small box on the counter and pushed it toward Linc.

"Your personal belongings from the office." Keaton shrugged. "Not that there was that much."

"Thanks." Linc didn't bother mentioning that his effort had been wasted.

"So," Keaton continued, "you're off tomorrow."

Linc considered ordering just one more drink, except that would be a mistake. "First thing in the a.m."

"I hate to lose you, but I can appreciate your need to move forward."

Linc had to laugh. "Actually, I'm moving backward."

Keaton waited for him to go on. He had accepted Linc's resignation without the usual notice. Linc appreciated that his former boss had turned out to be a stand-up guy. His help in taking down Marcos had been invaluable.

"Back to L.A.," Keaton acknowledged. "Perhaps, in time, you'll find that the move is forward after all."

Linc wasn't going to debate the issue. He was going back. To open the house. Take some time to figure out what he wanted to do next.

And wait for her to come back to him. Probably wishful thinking but he couldn't not do it. He still loved her as much as the day they'd married. That wasn't going to change this side of the grave.

"Call if you need a recommendation or anything else." Keaton stood. "Take care of yourself." He clapped Linc on the back and disappeared into the rowdy crowd.

Linc stared at the box. He couldn't just leave it

sitting there. Pulling it closer, he looked inside at
a pocket-size flashlight and a couple of unopened
letters. He rolled his eyes. Keaton had definitely
wasted his time. After tucking the mini flashlight
into his pocket, Linc picked up the two letters. The
first was junk mail from a spy equipment company.
The other was a medium-size padded envelope from
Mort, dated the day he'd died.

Linc's blood ran cold, then abruptly boiled. He
could care less what the bastard had to say...espe-
cially from the grave.

He ordered another drink.

By the time he'd finished off the absolutely last
drink he intended to have, his curiosity had gotten
the better of him. He ripped open the envelope and
removed a single sheet of plain white printer paper.
Mort's small, slanted handwriting filled the page.

Linc,
Yeah, I know. If I weren't already dead you'd
kill me. I don't blame you. What I did was
unforgivable. No question about that. Anyway,
I didn't write this letter to ask for your absolu-
tion. I did it for the money. Marcos needed
my help and I sold it to him. I was burned out,
in debt up to my eyeballs and feeling cheated
by the system. You were young and had your

whole life ahead of you. Lori wasn't expected to live. You were going to lose her anyway.

Once I'd crossed that line I couldn't take it back. I facilitated the bastard. Sent him the photos after you left and took care of all official records related to Lori. But you likely know all that by now. What you probably don't know is why Marcos wanted Lori. A young woman was on the yacht that day, Olivia Lopez. We all had her pegged as one of Marcos's women but we were wrong. As it turns out, he had a brother and this was his daughter. Because Marcos blamed himself for her death, he decided to take Lori from you. He gave her to his brother's wife to help her get past her only child's death.

What I did was unspeakable but that's not why I've cleaned my weapon and will soon be using it one last time. I have terminal cancer. With our conversation, I completed getting things in order, so to speak. Now I'm ready to go. I don't want to put my family through the pain or financial burden. Plus, I'm a coward. I haven't been a hero in a long time. Funny thing, I did hang on to a couple of items just in case. You'll find those enclosed. Good luck, buddy. I hope you nail the bastard.

Mort

Linc dropped the letter, his gut in knots, and pawed inside the envelope. He withdrew a small bag—an evidence bag. Inside was a clipping of brown hair and an ID card with photo and fingerprints.

Lorraine Reece.

Linc's hands shook as he smoothed the plastic so he could see more clearly. His pulse skipped. Lori's department ID card and a lock of her hair.

He smiled. This was all he needed to convince her that there was no doubt. She was his wife and she should come back to him.

No. He couldn't do that. When and if Lori wanted to be his wife again, she had to make that decision.

Linc had waited this long. He could wait forever if that was what it took.

Los Angeles, Sunday, July 17, 2:00 p.m.

MIA PAID THE TAXI DRIVER and thanked him. As he drove away, she stared up at the lovely old Victorian home. Two stories, with a broad, spacious wraparound porch. It was awesome. She might not remember but she knew she would have picked this house. She loved the two palm trees that adorned the yard, and the array of blooming plants.

She shifted the strap of her bag, clutched her purse to her chest and strode up the sidewalk to the porch. A gasp escaped her as she stood there staring upward. "Ceiling fans." There were two on the grand porch. Comfortable chairs and a well-worn hammock provided leisurely seating.

She absolutely loved it and she hadn't even been inside yet.

Mia took a deep breath and knocked on the door. She had been surprised when Mr. Keaton had told her that Linc had moved back to L.A. Then she'd gotten excited. This was perfect. She hoped he was home because she hadn't warned him she was coming.

A frown worried her brow when he didn't answer. Dang it. Then she noticed the doorbell and pressed it. Maybe he hadn't heard her knocking.

He had to be here.

Nineteen days with no contact. She had spent sixteen of those days at the recovery center the Colbys had recommended. With the help of the amazing people there she had come to a balanced decision about her future. It was time to put those decisions into action. She had packed up her things and put her bungalow in Blossom on the market. There were goodbyes that needed to be said and she'd said them. Now for the next step.

The door opened and he stood before her wearing the same kind of low-slung, faded jeans he always wore. She wasn't surprised that he was barefoot and shirtless. This was L.A. Casual was a religion.

"Hey."

That one word was all it took to make her heart flutter. She loved the husky sound of his voice. Loved his broad shoulders, that muscled chest and those lean hips. His eyes…his lips…his hair. Everything. She had dreamed of him every night.

She smiled. "Hey, to you."

He stepped back, opened the beautiful leaded-glass door wider. "Come in."

Mia crossed the threshold. Her senses went into overdrive. She couldn't take it all in. The man, the house. She turned around slowly in the center of the entry hall. This was home. Her gaze settled on Lincoln Reece. *He* was home.

"I want to see the rest." She let the bag drop to the floor and tossed her purse atop it.

Those deep, deep blue eyes lit with hope. He offered his hand. "Come on."

She put her hand in his and lost herself to his stories of how they'd found the house, renovated and decorated each room. Then they sat on the floor and spent hours going through boxes of photo albums.

And there it was…her life. Their life.

Linc closed the final album. "I have a few more boxes of framed photos to unpack."

"The house is awesome." She turned to him, couldn't get enough of looking at him. "You did good."

He shook his head. "You did good." He pointed to

the ceiling and then the walls. "You saw the before pictures. I would've walked away from the place. You had the vision."

"You have a point there," she agreed. The place had been a wreck. "Looks like we pulled it off together."

Silence lapsed comfortably between them. Mia closed her eyes and absorbed the pleasant vibes.

"The house is yours if you're ready to live here."

Mia opened her eyes, startled by his announcement.

"I had an inspector check all the mechanical systems and took care of any needed maintenance."

He spoke as if whatever she decided was fine by him, but that wasn't what she saw in his eyes. "What about you?" she asked. "Isn't this your house, too? Don't you want to stay?" She held her breath, prayed he hadn't given up and changed his mind.

That sadness she'd seen in his eyes the last time they were together made an appearance. "I want to stay."

A smile trembled across her lips. "Good. Because I want you to stay. This is our home."

He tucked a strand of hair behind her ear. She shivered. When he touched her nothing else mattered. "Are you sure about this?"

"Yes." She took his hand in hers. "I know this was

my life. I don't need any confirmation. This was our life and I want it back."

He reached up, caressed her cheek. "I want you back." The hope was back in his eyes. "I have proof now. A lock of your hair and your prints. Mort had been sitting on them all this time."

Mia leaned forward and kissed his waiting lips. "That's good but I don't need any additional evidence." She kissed him again. The taste of him made her want so much more. He had wanted to kiss her, too. She'd seen the desire in his eyes, but he'd waited for her to make the first move. She showed him with her lips just how much she wanted him. Let him feel the immensity of her desire to become intimately familiar with every part of him again. And again.

He was the one to slow things down, his breath as ragged as hers. "We don't have to be in a hurry," he murmured against her lips.

"There's just one part that's going to take some time," she murmured back. "Getting used to my real name." She had come to terms with returning to her birth name—the one that had been stolen from her. But it wouldn't be easy. She nipped his lip with her teeth. "But this—" she lavished the spot she'd teased with her tongue "—is like riding a bicycle. It comes back naturally."

"Excellent point." He started a path of slow, hot kisses down her throat.

She hung her arms around his neck, pulled him down to the floor and smiled up at him. "Let's make some memories."

Epilogue

Three months later

At sunrise the beach was deserted. The air was crisp and the ocean crashed against the rocks and sand like music set to accompany the glorious sunrise.

Linc held Lori's hands in his. She wore a gauzy, thin white dress with a necklace of pink flowers, just like the last time. He wore the same suit, the one she'd picked out. Navy to match the color of his eyes. The white shirt was a vivid contrast to the dark jacket, as was the single red rose tucked into his lapel.

He stared into her eyes and repeated the vows they had taken nine years ago. "To love and to cherish." He grinned. "Now and forever." He'd decided to change that last part. They'd already done the "until death do us part" thing.

Lori laughed, the sound like sweet bells tinkling

with the wash of the tide. She recited her vows, finishing with the same words he had used.

They kissed while the water swayed back and forth over their bare feet. The sand worked between his toes and made him smile against her lips. She laughed some more and he grabbed her around the waist and lifted her up against his chest.

"I love you, Mrs. Reece."

She kissed his nose. "I love you, Mr. Reece."

Two months ago she had started thinking of herself as Lori. She'd made her mark on the house. Moving pictures he had hung in the wrong places, she'd teased. Changing curtains and bedding she'd insisted were out of date.

"I'm hungry."

Linc whirled her around. She squealed. "We'll just have to do something about that."

"Good." She scooted out of his arms and righted her dress. "Because you're going to need plenty of energy." She winked and flitted toward the car.

He followed more slowly, content to watch her dance across the sand.

The first years of their life together were lost to her, but every day he reminded her with the photos and mementos of that time. Not one minute of this second chance would be taken for granted.

"Hurry, Linc!" She waved frantically from the passenger window.

He made sure that every day was filled with new memories.

They had a new plan, only this time they called it a nine-month plan instead of a five-year plan. Lori wanted a baby. Linc wanted at least two.

He climbed into the car and gave her a quick kiss.

She leaned over the console and kissed him hard. "Let's forget the food." She tugged at the top button of his shirt. "I want to make a baby."

Linc really liked this new plan.

* * * * *

INTRIGUE®

COMING NEXT MONTH

Available July 12, 2011

#1287 BY ORDER OF THE PRINCE
Cowboys Royale
Carla Cassidy

#1288 RUSTLED
Whitehorse, Montana: Chisholm Cattle Company
B.J. Daniels

#1289 COWBOY FEVER
Sons of Troy Ledger
Joanna Wayne

#1290 HER STOLEN SON
Guardian Angel Investigations: Lost and Found
Rita Herron

#1291 BAYOU BODYGUARD
Jana DeLeon

#1292 DEAL BREAKER
The McKenna Legacy
Patricia Rosemoor

You can find more information on upcoming
Harlequin® titles, free excerpts and more at
www.HarlequinInsideRomance.com.

HICNM0611

REQUEST YOUR FREE BOOKS!
2 FREE NOVELS PLUS 2 FREE GIFTS!

BREATHTAKING ROMANTIC SUSPENSE

YES! Please send me 2 FREE Harlequin Intrigue® novels and my 2 FREE gifts (gifts are worth about $10). After receiving them, if I don't wish to receive any more books, I can return the shipping statement marked "cancel." If I don't cancel, I will receive 6 brand-new novels every month and be billed just $4.24 per book in the U.S. or $4.99 per book in Canada. That's a saving of at least 15% off the cover price! It's quite a bargain! Shipping and handling is just 50¢ per book in the U.S. and 75¢ per book in Canada.* I understand that accepting the 2 free books and gifts places me under no obligation to buy anything. I can always return a shipment and cancel at any time. Even if I never buy another book, the two free books and gifts are mine to keep forever.

182/382 HDN FC5H

Name _____ (PLEASE PRINT) _____

Address _____ Apt. # _____

City _____ State/Prov. _____ Zip/Postal Code _____

Signature (if under 18, a parent or guardian must sign)

Mail to the Reader Service:
IN U.S.A.: P.O. Box 1867, Buffalo, NY 14240-1867
IN CANADA: P.O. Box 609, Fort Erie, Ontario L2A 5X3

Not valid for current subscribers to Harlequin Intrigue books.

**Are you a subscriber to Harlequin Intrigue books
and want to receive the larger-print edition?
Call 1-800-873-8635 or visit www.ReaderService.com.**

* Terms and prices subject to change without notice. Prices do not include applicable taxes. Sales tax applicable in N.Y. Canadian residents will be charged applicable taxes. Offer not valid in Quebec. This offer is limited to one order per household. All orders subject to credit approval. Credit or debit balances in a customer's account(s) may be offset by any other outstanding balance owed by or to the customer. Please allow 4 to 6 weeks for delivery. Offer available while quantities last.

Your Privacy—The Reader Service is committed to protecting your privacy. Our Privacy Policy is available online at www.ReaderService.com or upon request from the Reader Service.

We make a portion of our mailing list available to reputable third parties that offer products we believe may interest you. If you prefer that we not exchange your name with third parties, or if you wish to clarify or modify your communication preferences, please visit us at www.ReaderService.com/consumerschoice or write to us at Reader Service Preference Service, P.O. Box 9062, Buffalo, NY 14269. Include your complete name and address.

HI11

USA TODAY *bestselling author B.J. Daniels*
takes you on a trip to Whitehorse, Montana,
and the Chisholm Cattle Company.

RUSTLED

Available July 2011 from Harlequin Intrigue.

As the dust settled, Dawson got his first good look at the rustler. A pair of big Montana sky-blue eyes glared up at him from a face framed by blond curls.

A woman rustler?

"You have to let me go," she hollered as the roar of the stampeding cattle died off in the distance.

"So you can finish stealing my cattle? I don't think so." Dawson jerked the woman to her feet.

She reached for the gun strapped to her hip hidden under her long barn jacket.

He grabbed the weapon before she could, his eyes narrowing as he assessed her. "How many others are there?" he demanded, grabbing a fistful of her jacket. "I think you'd better start talking before I tear into you."

She tried to fight him off, but he was on to her tricks and pinned her to the ground. He was suddenly aware of the soft curves beneath the jean jacket she wore under her coat.

"You have to listen to me." She ground out the words from between her gritted teeth. "You have to let me go. If you don't they will come back for me and they will kill you. There are too many of them for you to fight off alone. You won't stand a chance and I don't want your blood on my hands."

"I'm touched by your concern for me. Especially after you just tried to pull a gun on me."

"I wasn't going to shoot you."

Dawson hauled her to her feet and walked her the rest of the way to his horse. Reaching into his saddlebag, he pulled out a length of rope.

"You can't tie me up."

He pulled her hands behind her back and began to tie her wrists together.

"If you let me go, I can keep them from coming back," she said. "You have my word." She let out an unladylike curse. "I'm just trying to save your sorry neck."

"And I'm just going after my cattle."

"Don't you mean your boss's cattle?"

"Those cattle are mine."

"*You're* a Chisholm?"

"Dawson Chisholm. And you are...?"

"Everyone calls me Jinx."

He chuckled. "I can see why."

*Bronco busting, falling in love...it's all in a day's work.
Look for the rest of their story in*

RUSTLED

*Available July 2011 from Harlequin Intrigue
wherever books are sold.*

SPECIAL EDITION

Life, Love and Family

THE TEXANS ARE COMING!

Reader-favorite miniseries Montana Mavericks
is back in Special Edition with new loves,
adventures and more.

July 2011 features *USA TODAY* bestselling author
CHRISTINE RIMMER
with
RESISTING MR. TALL, DARK & TEXAN.

A Texas oil mogul arrives in Thunder Canyon on
business and soon falls for his personal assistant. Only
one problem—she's just resigned to open a bakery!
Can he convince her to stay on—as his bride?

Find out in July!

Look for a new
Montana Mavericks: The Texans Are Coming title
in each of these months

| August | September | October |
| November | December | |

Available wherever books are sold.

UNRAVEL THE MYSTERY

HIDDEN WORDS:

Use the clues to solve these three-by-three word squares related to the house. When completed, the shaded diagonal will spell a hidden word that refers to space in the kitchen.

CLUES

1. Container, usually of metal, used for cooking.
2. Cooking pot, usually with a handle, for use on a stove.
3. Sealed metal container for food or drink.
4. Lidded container, or "____ can."
5. To cook something in fat.
6. A type of window.

FIND YOUR ANSWERS in next month's INTRIGUE titles, available July 12!